For a mom[ent] [...]
he'd fallen head over heels in love with.

He wanted to pull her into his arms and assure her that everything was going to be all right. But he couldn't promise that since he wasn't sure he knew this woman as well as he'd once thought.

Seeing her again had knocked him off-kilter. He hadn't expected her to come back to Montana— let alone here, so close to Fortune Creek and him. And now she was mixed up dead center in his investigation.

Determined to keep this official and not dig through the past, he pulled out his notebook. "Tell me again how you ended up in Starling."

Olivia blinked as if she hadn't expected him to ask about the investigation.

"Nice to see you, too, Jaden. Yes, I'm glad to be home. No, I wish I hadn't run into old high school friends and decided to go with them out to Starling on Halloween."

ENGAGING
THE DEPUTY

B.J. DANIELS

Harlequin

INTRIGUE

There is nothing like the people you grew up with in a small town in Montana. It's like a family. Sometimes a dysfunctional family that can become dangerous—at least in this book.

This one is for those who remember West Yellowstone and Rainbow Point in the 1960s.

Harlequin® INTRIGUE™

ISBN-13: 978-1-335-45744-8

Engaging the Deputy

Harlequin Enterprises ULC
22 Adelaide St. West, 41st Floor
Toronto, Ontario M5H 4E3, Canada
www.Harlequin.com

Printed in Lithuania

Recycling programs for this product may not exist in your area.

MIX
Paper | Supporting responsible forestry
FSC® C021394

New York Times and *USA TODAY* bestselling author **B.J. Daniels** lives in Montana with her husband, Parker, and three springer spaniels. When not writing, she quilts, boats and plays tennis. Contact her at bjdaniels.com, on Facebook or on X @bjdanielsauthor.

Visit the Author Profile page at Harlequin.com.

CAST OF CHARACTERS

Deputy Sheriff Jaden Montgomery—His former fiancée was not only back in Montana, but in the middle of his murder investigation?

Olivia Brooks—She'd come home following her heart only to get caught in a tornado—and a murder investigation by her ex-fiancé.

Cody Ryan—He had to believe his high school sweetheart and once best friend had returned home because of him.

Rob Perkins—His secrets had literally gotten him killed.

Dean Marsh—He wasn't a great husband, but like his wife said, he wasn't a killer—or was he?

Angie Marsh—She'd had enough of Dean. She was moving on.

Jenny Lee—She'd put herself in a bad place by still being in love with Dean.

Emery Jordan—The bike shop owner didn't want trouble—especially not from his friends.

Chapter One

Ghostlike shapes of abandoned houses appeared on the darkening skyline ahead. Olivia Brooks had been nervous enough about this night but now felt a sense of foreboding she couldn't shake off. Why had she agreed to this? She hated this place and especially this fool idea of how to spend Halloween night. The settlement of Starling, Montana, was desolate and deserted, the anti-government group long gone but not forgotten. She hadn't liked the way it made her feel in the daylight, let alone late at night.

"The graves of lost dreams," her date said next to her in the back seat of his friend Dean's king-cab pickup. As Cody Ryan looked out his side window at what was left of Starling, she remembered why she'd agreed to this Halloween date. She'd missed Cody. He'd been the boy next door, her best buddy growing up, her high school sweetheart. When she thought of him, she thought of home.

The idea of spending time with him had appealed to her maybe more than it should have since it hadn't been all that long ago that she'd been engaged to someone else. She'd come home to heal. She'd missed having a friend whom she shared a childhood with. Now that she was home again, Cody was a huge part of those memories. Mostly, she missed the closeness they'd once shared as kids.

"Slow down," Jenny ordered Dean from the front seat of the pickup as he took a curve too fast on the narrow road. Weeds that had grown up between the two dirt tracks scraped the bottom of the truck like fingernails down a blackboard.

Olivia and Cody exchanged a look. Dean and Jenny both seemed tense, not that they didn't have every reason to be. She wondered whose idea this date had been, given they both were married to someone else.

Behind them, the headlight beams of the second vehicle suddenly filled the pickup's cab as Dean hit the brakes and came to a dust-boiling stop. Emery Jordan laid on his van's horn as he roared up, barely stopping before crashing into the back of the truck.

"Just like old times," Cody said, shaking his head as he looked over at her. He didn't sound as if he was enjoying this any more than she was. They'd run into each other at the local bar in town last night. Olivia had been the outlier, going away to college and not coming back for six years.

At the bar, they'd all been drinking and laughing about old times. She hadn't realized how much she'd missed this hometown comradery, especially with Cody. She hadn't talked to him since they'd broken up when she'd left for college. Like most of their other friends, he hadn't left the small Montana town. He'd been working at his father's local hardware store for as long as she could remember.

That night at the bar, being around old friends, especially Cody, felt so right that she'd questioned why she'd ever left. He looked the same but different in a good way. Mostly, he felt familiar and comforting, like finding an old worn flannel shirt she'd forgotten about that still fit perfectly.

Talking at the bar, it was as if they'd never been apart. When he'd asked her to come with him tonight, along with several of their old friends all now in their twenties, it felt almost as if she could rewrite history. She'd often wondered what her life would have been like if she had never left.

Inviting her must have seemed like a good idea at the time, even though Cody didn't seem so sure now that they were out there, especially when Rob's plan was that they all had to stay until midnight. Their friend Rob Perkins had been celebrating the other night at the bar. He'd been offered a really good position in Seattle. He was excited about the condo he'd purchased on the coast and this opportunity to change his life.

"Let's do something epic on Halloween," he'd said.

"Let's go to Starling!" Emery Jordan had said and thrown an arm around Rob.

"Great idea," Rob had agreed and grinned. "Let's go look for the gold." Everyone had groaned at even the mention of the legend—let alone going out to the abandoned community. Folklore claimed that the anti-government leader and founder of the Starling community, Elden Rusk, had taken all of his followers' money, converted it into gold and hidden it somewhere in the town before his mysterious disappearance. The gold, if it had existed, had reputedly never been found.

"But we have to stay until midnight," Rob had said. "That's when the really scary stuff happens. Unless you're all chicken," he'd taunted. Never the kind to back down from a dare, especially when they'd all had a couple of beers, their old group had quickly agreed. It was a date.

Olivia had looked to Cody, who'd given her that familiar grin. "What do you think?" he'd asked.

She'd nodded, warmed by the alcohol and her old friends. There was nothing quite like the people she'd grown up with, the boys she'd dated, the friends she'd known, the memories they'd made. She'd been the dreamer, determined to go to college, to have a career, not to end up like her mother had.

Six years ago, her friends hadn't understood her need to chase her dream—especially Cody, she thought as she looked out at Starling, unsure now what they were doing there together.

As they exited the truck into the darkness, she was having misgivings. She didn't want to give Cody the wrong impression. She wasn't interested in taking up where they'd left off. She just wanted that boy-next-door friend she'd missed.

Rob and Emery and their dates piled out of the van, shouting and yelling. She saw that Emery was helping Rob unload a cooler full of beer from the back of the van and realized what those two had planned.

Emery and Rob had brought dates as well, although the women were much younger than Olivia and the old crowd. Tammy and Whitney had their heads together, giggling over something. Clearly, that carload had been drinking on the drive out to the middle of nowhere and the remains of the Starling community.

"Okay, whoever finds the gold, remember, we split it," Rob said, laughing. "Except for anyone who wimps out before midnight."

Olivia took the beer Cody handed her and popped the top as they all stood around the cooler for a few moments. Rob and Emery retrieved their dates and headed down the hillside to some of the houses along the creek. She could hear Rob relating the story of Starling and its tragic end with relish as they went off to explore the dozen structures scattered across the hillside.

Jenny and Dean sat on the tailgate of his pickup, engrossed in each other even though married to other people. She saw that Dean had brought the mattress from his front porch futon and put it in the bed of the pickup. Seemed everyone had something in mind tonight. This wasn't going anything like she'd expected.

"Take a walk?" Cody asked as if as uncomfortable as she was. At the bar, they'd all been having fun together. Now they had broken off into real dates.

With growing discomfort, she walked away from the vehicles with Cody. It felt as though the bad part of their past had been hiding out here in the dark, waiting for them. The skeletal remains of one of the weather-beaten houses rose before them, etched against the night sky. She didn't want to think about the last time she'd seen Cody before she'd left town. They'd argued. She knew that she'd hurt him and hated that. But she also knew that was why she'd stayed away so long.

The air felt heavy, as if a storm was blowing in. Clouds scudded past as silent as wispy ghosts and blotted out the stars and moon, making the night darker than usual. Gusts of wind caught her long blond hair, lashing it across her face. She grabbed a handful and forced it into a ponytail with the scrunchie she'd brought.

"Aren't you worried that we might see the ghost of Evangeline?" she asked and took a sip of her beer, the eerie hillside scene making her jumpy as much as Cody's silence. She felt him glance at her as if he understood what she was doing. He knew her better than most anyone because of all those years they'd been inseparable.

"She probably ran away," Cody said. "Had enough of small-town living. Wanted something better."

She shot him a look. Was he really going to bring up her leaving now? She sighed, knowing that she couldn't explain why she'd had to leave when she had or why she hadn't come back. He hadn't understood six years ago. Why would he now? "The teen years are tough. Who knows what we want at that age?"

"I always knew what I wanted."

Olivia groaned inwardly and pulled her coat a little tighter around her as if the temperature had suddenly dropped. "You were lucky."

"Lucky? Right," he said without looking at her as they walked. "My dream was to work in my father's hardware store my entire life. Some of us couldn't just leave."

The wind picked up, stronger now. She could hear clanging metal on metal in the distance. Closer, a windmill's sails moaned as they spun restlessly, several of the blades broken or missing altogether.

She swallowed, feeling Cody's disappointment and hurt and wishing she could take it away as she took in the derelict-looking structure ahead. If he was being truthful, he hadn't wanted to go to college. He probably hadn't even wanted to leave. He'd always felt as if he were trapped here, but if he'd wanted something else badly enough, wouldn't he have found a way?

Olivia had put herself through college. It wasn't like her mother had been able to help. She tried to change the subject, not wanting to argue with him.

"Elden Rusk had a dream," she said, thinking of her own. "He wanted a little different life," she said without looking at Cody. "There's nothing wrong with chasing a dream."

"Yep," he agreed. "Had great plans for the future, sold everyone on building this community, putting all their hopes and dreams into it, thinking this would be their home. Then he up and bails on them—"

"His sixteen-year-old daughter disappeared." She was losing her patience with him.

"Or just took off. Either way, the Starling dream died when he abandoned his flock." He held up his hands to encompass the dark houses of Starling and their lost hope. "'Sorry,' he says, 'but I'm moving on.'"

"I'm sure it was very painful for him to leave like he did," she observed, hoping this would be the end of their discussion since they weren't talking about Elden Rusk. "He must have been brokenhearted, not just for his daughter, but his community and friends he had to leave behind."

She stopped walking and felt a chill as the deep shadow of what she recognized as Elden Rusk's house loomed in front of them. She remembered when this house had been in all the newspapers and on the television news. She wished they hadn't walked this way. Just as she wished they hadn't had to do a postmortem on their high school relationship after all this time.

Cody turned to her. "What happened with us, Olivia? I never thought you'd leave, let alone walk away from what I thought we were building together."

His voice was so filled with anguish, she wished there was something she could say.

"I used to talk about my dreams with you," she said.

He kicked at the dirt at his feet. The wind caught it and whirled it around them. "You just didn't mention that I wasn't part of them."

"Is this why you invited me out here tonight?" she asked, her voice cracking. "Cody, we used to be friends. I thought… It's why I came along tonight. I didn't realize everyone was going to go their separate ways."

"You didn't realize it was a date," he said and sighed. They stood only inches apart. He seemed to study her as if he'd never seen her before. "I thought I could do this, pretend you and I never happened, just be friends, no hard feelings." He shook his head. "Sorry, but I can't."

Her eyes burned with tears. "You picked a great time to get that off your chest," she said, determined not to cry. "It isn't like we can just get in the car and leave now." Glancing back, she could no longer see Jenny and Dean or the tailgate anymore. Had they moved to the futon bed? Probably. Not the best time to go down there and ask for a ride back to town. "I don't know what you want me to say," she said, turning to him. "I'm sorry."

"I guess I always believed you'd come back to me," Cody said. "Even as kids, and later as teenagers, you and I were so close. I thought we'd end up together, that I would prove to you I'm the right man for you. I'm not going to work in that hardware store the rest of my life." He shook his head. "You never had any faith in me, but you know what the worst part is? After you left, I ran into Deputy Jaden Montgomery, the guy you fell for in college. We had a nice conversation."

She groaned. "Are we really getting into this now out here?"

"Maybe we should since I hadn't realized that the two of you had been *engaged* and apparently you broke his heart too. Now I'm wondering how many others there have been."

"Don't be ridiculous," she snapped. "You and I—"

They both started at the sound of a bloodcurdling scream followed by a burst of laughter and shrieks. Down the hillside, between the dark outlines of two houses, she saw Rob chasing either Tammy or Whitney, she couldn't tell which. But when she looked back, Cody was about to enter Elden's house.

For just an instant, she thought about going back to the

truck, as embarrassing as it could have been. But she didn't want to go alone. She told herself that she could make it until midnight if Cody could. She hurried to catch up to him as the wind whirled dust around her. Ahead, she heard a door creak open.

Chapter Two

Cody wished he'd kept his mouth shut. He was mentally kicking himself for bringing up the past. He'd asked her to come along tonight because he'd missed her. He'd planned to keep it casual. Old friends. Nothing more.

Unfortunately, being around Olivia had brought back all the good memories from their childhood. She'd been his first real love. Maybe it had been puppy love, but it had been real to him. He'd really thought they would end up together; he always had.

He'd thought she'd felt the same way, not that they had ever talked about the future in high school. He hadn't realized he wasn't in her future until she'd dropped the bombshell. Not only was she going far away to college, but also she was breaking up with him. He'd never understand how she could leave seventeen years of life and all those memories and not look back, but she had.

So, what was she doing back in town?

When he'd seen her walk into the bar the other day, he'd realized that he'd never given up on his fantasy of the two of them being together. How could he not have thought it was meant to be? She had returned. She'd agreed to come out here tonight with him. But that was where the fantasy ended, he thought. They weren't kids anymore, let alone high school sweethearts. She just wanted to be friends. He swore under his breath. Maybe it was just as well, he told himself.

Standing inside the house, Cody hadn't heard her come up behind him—not with the wind whistling through the broken glass of the windows. He jumped when she touched his shoulder. He had stepped into Elden Rusk's dark house and stopped, realizing belatedly how dangerous this was as he felt the floor give under him. He couldn't see anything in the pitch blackness. For all he knew, part of the floor had caved in and he might step into the abyss.

"Don't come any closer," he warned as he pulled a penlight from his pocket. He wished he'd brought something larger and brighter. The LED beam did little to chase away the shadows from the dark corners.

At one window, a ragged white curtain suddenly billowed, making Olivia grab his hand as she let out a surprised cry. They stood like that, her hand warm in his. They could have been kids again standing there. But they weren't.

"I'm sorry," he whispered. He regretted spoiling this night and the time he had with her. He wasn't sure what had brought her back to town, but it wasn't him. He doubted she would be staying long. "Want to get out of here?" Her shoulder was against his, so he felt her nod and turned them back toward the open door they'd come through.

As they stepped outside, she let go of his hand. He wasn't sure what they could do to kill time until midnight. He'd be glad when they'd finally be able to leave. This idea of a "date" had been a mistake.

"We could search for the buried gold," she said, clearly only half-serious. Like him, she was probably looking for anything to do until midnight, when they could go their separate ways. He had a pretty good idea of what the other couples were doing as he glanced back toward the vehicles. Dean and Jenny were probably still down there getting into trouble. Cody had been surprised and upset when Dean had told him Jenny was coming along.

"Where's her husband?" Cody had asked, hating to mention the obvious.

"Out of town. Angie's at her mother's. Don't say it. I know, but I never got over Jenny. If anyone should understand not being able to move on, it should be you."

Cody had let it go, realizing it was true. He hadn't moved on. Instead, he'd been stuck, as if he hadn't wanted to see a future without Olivia. As they'd swung by to pick up the two women before heading out to Starling, he'd realized that he'd been waiting for Olivia to return. He'd never seen himself settling down with anyone else.

Now he knew that it wasn't just Dean who was doing something foolish tonight. Standing in the creaking old house on the hillside in Starling, he knew he had been deluding himself. His wanting to believe that he had no future without Olivia had really been him not facing that he'd wasted years working at the hardware store with his father, waiting for his life to finally begin. Seeing her again had brought the realization home that it was time to change things. That was what he'd been working toward. Now it was time.

He finished the beer he'd been holding and tossed the empty can into the darkness of the house. A strong gust of wind howled off the eaves, pelting them with dirt. "Why not look for gold inside the houses?" he said. "Anything to get out of this wind." They dropped off the hill to the closest small dwelling below the founder's so much larger one.

He noticed Olivia glance at the dark shape of Rusk's house looming over the town. She looked as if she'd been expecting to see Elden Rusk standing in the doorway, watching them go. Another of the local legends out here at Starling was the alleged sighting of Elden's ghost searching for his daughter. Wandering around at night calling "Evangeline!" as he stumbled, heartbroken, through the deserted town.

Cody didn't believe any of it. If there had been any gold, he'd bet Rusk had taken it with him.

OLIVIA FELT A CHILL she couldn't quite throw off. After they'd walked away from the Rusk house, she'd sensed someone watching them and had turned to look back. Enough light had sifted through the clouds to illuminate a dark figure in what looked like a long black coat, wearing a floppy black hat, standing in the doorway they'd just deserted. In the blink of an eye, the image was gone as if it had never been there.

She shuddered, telling herself she'd imagined seeing the figure of Elden Rusk, and blamed the creepy place, the dark night and being back here, maybe especially with Cody. She hated the tension she felt between them. All that talk about Rusk and the past was making her see things.

She caught up with Cody, and they entered the small house. The door had been standing open. Cody turned on his penlight. Like the Rusk house, most of the windows appeared to be missing.

They'd only just stepped in when a shriek filled the night air from a house farther down by the creek where they'd last seen Rob and Emery and their dates. Everyone seemed to be enjoying themselves, Olivia thought. She wished she hadn't left her purse with her phone in Dean's truck. She had no idea what time it was, but feared midnight was still hours away.

She and Cody had barely gotten inside the house when a gust of wind literally shook the walls around them. Cody went to one of the glassless windows to look out. She could hear a distant howl, the sound seeming to grow in strength as the wind picked up even more.

"This is going to be some storm," he said, sounding nervous as another squall shook the house. "Do you hear that?"

Earlier, all she could hear were the creaks and groans of the walls, the whistles of the wind through the broken panes. But now she could hear what sounded like a roar. She hugged herself, just wanting to get out of the house, out of Starling.

"We should round up the others and head back," she suggested. Ending this outing early seemed like the best idea, given the way this night was going, especially with a bad storm brewing.

"I don't think there's time," Cody said, turning from the window, the beam of his penlight illuminating a spot on the floor at his feet. She could see his expression. "I think we'd better find a safe place to ride it out."

Seriously? "Doesn't it make more sense to go back to the pickup?" she asked, but he didn't seem to be listening. The house shuddered as the wind grew stronger, the howling sound louder. Dirt peppered the side of the structure as Cody moved toward her, his expression making her more anxious. The house shuddered again. "Cody?"

"When I was a boy at my grandmother's, we had to go into the root cellar because of a tornado." He had to yell to be heard. She remembered him telling her the story. "I think this might be a tornado. That's what it sounds like."

"That was Oklahoma. We don't have tornadoes like that in Montana, do we?"

"Come on. No matter what it is, we're finding a safe

place until it's over." He grabbed her hand and led her deeper inside. He shone his light on the floor as they moved farther into the house until they reached the old kitchen.

"What are you looking for?" she yelled over the howl outside. The wind rattled the walls, shaking the floor under them.

"A root cellar. I think every house up here had one where they kept their canned goods from their gardens." He moved the little flashlight beam around the floor until he found what he was looking for. "There it is. The trapdoor. Here, hold the light."

Standing back, the light making a small pool on the surface, she watched him reach into a slight indentation in the floorboards and pull. The wood groaned and creaked. It seemed to take all his strength, but finally he lifted the door, exposing a wooden ladder that dropped down into total blackness.

A musty, decayed smell rose as she watched Cody brush away cobwebs before reaching for the penlight again. "I'll check it out," he shouted over the deafening roar. The house shook. "We have to hurry!"

She could hear what sounded like objects hitting the walls on the outside. Not dirt or pebbles like earlier—large things that crashed against the side of the house.

He disappeared down the ladder. She moved to the edge of the hole that had been dug into the dirt beneath the house. She shivered at the thought of going down there, even as she heard what sounded like houses being turned into kindling. When she looked toward the glassless window, she saw large debris flying past.

"Cody?" she cried an instant before he reached up for her.

"Take my hand. Hurry."

She grasped his hand, falling into his arms. She'd barely dropped down a couple of rungs next to him when he slammed the trapdoor and locked it. Overhead, there was a loud crash that sounded as if the house had caved in.

"CODY?" HER VOICE came out breathless, making him think of when he'd been able to make her sound like that simply by kissing her.

"You're okay," he said as he slipped down the ladder and reached up to help her. They stood in utter darkness. He had the sense that he could no longer tell up from down. Snapping on his penlight, he saw her expression. She looked so vulnerable, so terrified. It reminded him of when they'd been kids and he'd been there for her; the few times he'd been braver than her.

He could see that she'd never been in a root cellar before and hadn't been anxious to enter into this one. He hadn't been either. Now he just hoped that he'd made the right decision. "I'll clean you off a place to sit."

He picked up a board that might have been part of the shelving system at one point and dusted off the dirt and cobwebs. "Here, sit on this."

She descended the last few steps and stood for a moment, clearly not wanting to sit at all. He knew the feeling. He watched her glance around, wide-eyed, in the faint glow of the penlight, making him think of that time at his grandmother's. There had been something terrifying about running out of the house in the middle of the night to crawl into a dirt hole in the ground. He recalled the panic he'd felt when his grandfather had closed the door and locked it.

Over their heads, the thundering had increased in volume, sounding now like a locomotive barreling down on them.

"What's happening?" she asked, her voice small in the

contained space. The root cellar was tiny compared to his grandmother's. There were only two sets of heavy-looking wooden shelves with a couple of jars of canned goods on each. He pulled out more boards for them, knowing they would have to wait out the storm.

"We could be here for a while, though, so let's sit, okay?"

She lowered herself to the boards and he joined her, more concerned about what was happening over their heads than he wanted her to know.

"It's a tornado." He could hear what sounded like the town ripping apart over their heads, but down here, it was relatively quiet. "I know it's rare, but I've heard of tornadoes in Montana. Usually, they're fairly small." This one didn't sound small at all.

She swallowed and looked as worried as he felt. "What if we're buried alive down here?" she whispered as if he hadn't thought of that.

"I think we're safer here," he said as he put a protective arm around her. It had to be a tornado. He couldn't imagine a thunderstorm doing the kind of damage they were hearing above them—not in Montana, where he'd lived his entire life. Rare windstorms tore off roofs, rolled over semis on the highway, swept in blizzards that closed all the roads out of town, but what was happening outside sounded as if the entire community of Starling was in the extremes of being leveled.

Just when he thought it couldn't get any louder or stronger, it did. The clatter was suddenly deafening. He tentatively tightened his arm around her and was glad when she curled against him, burying her face in his shoulder.

But when he looked up, he saw the boards being ripped off the kitchen floor. He pulled her down to the dirt floor, covering her body with his own. He could feel the wind pulling at his clothing, at his body, as if preparing to lift them both out of the earth and into the whirling maelstrom over their heads.

She cried out as he grabbed the heavy shelving unit and toppled it onto them to help hold them down, holding on to her as the house above them splintered apart.

"Don't worry. I won't let you go," he cried over the noise, wishing he hadn't six years ago. He wasn't that man anymore, but he had no more chance of hanging on to her now than he did then as the floor over them disappeared.

THE SILENCE WAS suddenly deafening. "Olivia?" For a moment, Cody feared she wouldn't answer because she wasn't just buried under the debris and him—she was dead.

He felt her move under him. "Hold on," he said as he pushed the shelf off them, along with his weight on her. "Are you okay?"

"I think so," she said tentatively.

Cody sat up, shaking off the dirt and debris as he turned to look at her. Like him, she was filthy, but she looked unharmed.

"What was that?" she whispered.

"Definitely a tornado." They were still down on the ground, but there was a gapingly huge hole above them instead of the house's floor and once closed and locked trapdoor. He could see starlight overhead.

He could also see that part of the ladder to climb out was missing. He turned on the penlight and shone it around the space. Lowering the light, he looked at Olivia and found himself smiling.

"What?" she demanded, reaching up to pull a sliver of wood from her hair.

"You… Your face is a little dirty, that's all," he lied. "I must look filthy too."

She pushed to her feet. Her blue eyes were wide with the fear that still had her in its grip.

"We're alive," he said and laughed. "That was something, wasn't it?"

He saw her swallow and look skyward. "I need out of here."

"That might require some help. I'm not sure about the ladder," he was saying as she grabbed hold of it and the rung tore off.

"Easy," he said as another part of the ladder fell away from the dirt wall, sending debris onto them. Fortunately, he caught the ladder before it hit him in the head.

"You have to be kidding," she said, sounding close to tears.

"Don't worry. I'll figure something out," he said as he noticed something he hadn't before. A portion of the root cellar behind Olivia had caved in. With the storm past, he'd just been glad that neither of them had been injured. But now he worried that the rest of the cellar might not be stable. They still could be buried alive if they weren't careful.

"Why don't you move over here by me?" he said as his light caught on a pile of something white lying in the caved-in portion of the cellar. "Easy," he warned again.

"If you're trying to scare me—"

The moment she reached him, he got a clear view of the bones that had been exposed when a portion of the wall had caved in.

"What is that?" Olivia cried, moving even closer to him as she took in his grisly discovery. "Are they…*human bones*?"

Chapter Three

Deputy Jaden Montgomery was already out assessing the damage left behind from the windstorm. Power was non-existent in some areas and there was reported damage to a few buildings, including a couple of old barns that had lost their roofs. But no injuries or loss of life.

Until he got the frantic call from Starling.

"We need help!" Emery Jordan had cried. "We're out here in Starling, what's left of it. I can't find Rob. I can't find the others. Oh, man, it's really bad here. The town is almost completely gone. The tornado…" His voice had broken.

"How many of you are out there?" Jaden had asked and then told Emery to sit tight, that he was on his way. Starling was the last place on earth he wanted to go on Halloween night, of all nights. He had enough bad memories of the place. His parents had been members of the anti-government militant group years ago, long before Elden Rusk had left and the community had scattered, some a lot farther than Fortune Creek, where he now lived.

He had no desire to recall one of the darkest times of his childhood and had avoided going anywhere near Starling. He knew teenagers often went out there in an attempt to scare themselves with the ghost stories and alleged sightings of Elden Rusk. Kids! But Emery Jordan wasn't a kid anymore. What had a bunch of them been doing out there at their ages?

As he drove toward the abandoned community, the closer he got, the more eerie it felt. But he hadn't expected almost total destruction. In his headlights, he began to see the piles of debris the storm had left, houses leveled to the ground. It looked as if a bomb had gone off, turning some buildings to kindling and sending others hurling off their foundations to pile up a quarter mile away.

The devastation shocked him, not that he hadn't hoped years ago that the place would disappear forever. Reports of a tornado had come in late last night. But they usually did little more than tear up a barn or shed, wipe out a few telephone poles.

The brunt of the storm had missed Fortune Creek, yet had pretty much wiped Starling off the map, from what he could see in the moonlight. According to Emery, he and seven other twentysomethings from the closest town of Libby had been partying in the empty buildings when the storm had hit. Right now, five of them were missing and others had minor injuries.

Jaden had called in medical help as well as a search party on his way to the scene. As he came over the rise, he saw a van sitting sideways in the road and a pickup lying on its side, buried in debris. What appeared to be the roof of a house had piled up beside the road.

A bad feeling settled in his stomach as he parked and got out.

OLIVIA SCREAMED. SHE WOULD have kept screaming for help, but Cody pulled her to him in a tight hug.

"No one can hear us down here," he said. "Do you have your phone?"

She shook her head, her mind whirling like the tornado. They were trapped in a dirt hole with human bones. It was too easy to imagine her own bones decaying down here when no one found them. She was trying so hard not to cry, not to panic, but it was useless. She'd never been so terrified.

"I left my phone in the truck," Cody said. It was still dark outside, except for the stars and moonlight. She had no idea what time it was without her phone. Why had she left it and her purse in the truck? Because they'd only been going for a walk? Who'd known a tornado would hit and they'd end up almost buried alive in an old root cellar?

She shivered, avoiding looking at the pile of bones as she tried to pull herself together. "You think it's Evangeline Rusk?" Olivia asked, her voice trembling.

Cody shook his head. "It could be anybody."

"Hello!" she called, her voice echoing, her throat raspy. "Anyone out there? We need help!" No answer.

It didn't help that Cody was trying so hard to reassure her. "Someone will come looking for us."

"If anyone is still alive." Her eyes burned with tears.

"Let's just keep our cool. I'll see about using some of the shelves as a ladder, but we have to be careful, so we don't make the dirt cave in any more, okay?"

She nodded, trying not to think about the rest of the dirt walls toppling down on them.

"Hey," he said, putting his hands on both of her shoulders. "Breathe. You're fine. You're here with me."

Her vision blurred but she nodded again. His words both soothed and hurt. Earlier, Cody had been angry with her, unforgiving. But he'd saved her during the storm. Probably saved her life by insisting they find a place to ride out the storm. He was still trying to protect her. "I'm so sorry," she cried.

"You're okay. We're okay." He held her tighter.

"You saved my life," she said, sobbing into his shoulder.

"Not yet," he said. "Come on." He pulled back to look into her eyes before taking the tail of his shirt and gently wiping her face. "Even now, you look beautiful."

She scoffed but made an effort to stop crying. She'd always prided herself on her strength and determination. Where was that woman right now?

"Can I help you with the shelves?"

He smiled. "That's the girl I used to know," he said. "Too bad we found old bones instead of the gold."

The silence was getting to her. Where were the others? Suddenly, she was even more afraid. "What if everyone is—"

"Hey," he said. "They're probably just like us, digging themselves out."

"Sure." Except she didn't believe it. It was too quiet.

As HE WALKED up the road, Jaden spotted three of the survivors huddled together by the van. They were some distance from the demolished community, as if wanting to be as far away from it as possible. The largest of the group rose as he approached. He recognized Emery Jordan, but not the two young women with him. They were all filthy—their faces blackened with dirt, their clothing torn and dirty—but they didn't appear too badly hurt.

Emery, he saw, had what appeared to be superficial cuts and bruises, except for the one leg he was favoring. Mostly, he looked scared as the deputy walked toward him.

Jaden felt the weight of the quiet that had settled over the place. It made his skin crawl.

As he reached them, the two young women began to cry, holding tight to each other. "My mother's going to kill me," the brunette sobbed.

Seeing that they didn't appear to need medical attention, Jaden pulled out his notebook and took down their names, Tammy Bell and Whitney Clark. Both were underage to have been at a party where alcohol had obviously been served. Both said they had already called home and their parents were on their way to get them.

"I can't find Rob," Emery said. "He was there one minute and then…" He put his head in his hands.

"Give me the names of the others with you," Jaden said.

"Cody Ryan and Olivia Brooks. Rob Per—"

"Olivia Brooks?" Jaden stopped him. "She's back in town?" This was definitely news to him.

"Yeah, she's back," Emery said, sounding like it was no big deal. Probably wasn't to him, but then, he'd never been engaged to her. "Rob Perkins, Dean Marsh and Jenny Lee."

"Where was the last time you saw the others?" the deputy asked.

"Cody and Olivia went off that way," Emery said, waving toward what was left standing of Elden Rusk's house on the side of the hill. "Jenny Lee and Dean Marsh were here at the truck. Rob Perkins and I and the girls went down by the creek." His voice broke with emotion. "I thought we were all going to die."

Jaden looked up the hillside to where Emery had last seen Olivia headed. Even from this distance, he could see that only some of Elden Rusk's house was still standing, while the one just below it on the hill, where Jaden and his family had lived, was completely gone.

He desperately wanted to go looking for Olivia himself, but three other vehicles arrived. He needed to talk to the EMTs and search and rescue personnel. Too many people were still missing.

"DID YOU HEAR THAT?" Olivia whispered as she lifted one end of the heavy shelves and turned them to stand against the wall of dirt. "Voices."

He'd heard the voices and was as anxious as she was to get out of this root cellar. "It's probably the others."

"Maybe someone called for help," she said excitedly.

"Told you we would be found."

"But we aren't staying down here until they do, right?"

He shook his head. That was definitely not part of his plan for the night. "I'm going to help you climb out. Just stay low when you get near the top. Lie on your belly and crawl away from the edge so it doesn't cave in any more than it has." All he needed was for her to topple this damn hole on top of him.

She looked scared again. "You're going to be right behind me, aren't you?"

"Right behind you," he assured her, hoping that the shelves held enough to get her free. "Once you're out, head for the road we drove in on. If someone called for backup, that's where they'll be."

"I'm not leaving you down here," she said.

"Olivia—" He cursed under his breath. How had he forgotten how stubborn she could be?

"No. I might have left you once, but not again. Especially not like this." She shook her head adamantly. "We're both leaving here together."

He didn't want to argue, so he agreed. He didn't want to waste the time. The root-cellar walls felt unstable. He didn't think either of them should stay down there any longer than they had to.

"I'm going to be right behind you," he told her. "Just climb up and out. Don't look back."

She mugged a face at him, and for a moment, he thought she was hesitating because there was something she needed to say to him. "There's plenty of time to talk when we're out of here, okay?"

She nodded, grabbed hold of the old shelving and, with his hands guiding her upward, climbed, not hesitating, and was up and out before several of the wood shelves broke apart. The nails used to hold the boards together had barely held with her light weight.

Not a good sign, he was thinking when he realized that she'd just disappeared over the edge of the hole when she appeared again. She'd taken off her coat and, lying on her stomach, was dangling it over the side. "Your turn," she said, a dark silhouette against the lightening skyline.

"The shelves aren't going to hold me. I can hear rescuers. Go get some help." He didn't mean to snap, but he knew the clock was ticking and she was determined not to leave him. If only she'd felt that way six years ago. "Go! Please. I'll wait right here for you."

She hadn't been gone but a few moments before he moved the last shelving unit over against the wall. He hadn't told Olivia, but the last thing he planned to do was stay down there if he could help it. He could hear crying and someone calling Rob's name.

His weight broke the first shelf right away, but he'd gotten high enough that he could see over the rim of the root cellar in time to glimpse a dark figure move past. He started to call out but stopped himself. The person wasn't going for help—but in the opposite direction, deeper into the nearly-destroyed Starling community.

Just before disappearing from sight, the figure turned, as if looking back in Cody's direction. Cody dropped out of sight, hoping he hadn't been seen. He was trapped in this hole. If anyone wanted to harm him, it would be like shooting fish in a bucket.

ONCE JADEN GAVE the information he had to search and rescue, they began grabbing their gear.

He turned to Emery. "How did you and Rob get separated?"

Emery wiped his nose and looked down the hillside. "Whitney and I went over to that small house by the creek to give him and Tammy some privacy."

Jaden looked to Tammy, who was huddled with Whitney on a large boulder beside the road. "You were with Rob when the storm hit?"

"We'd been visiting down by the water. I got scared and went to find Whit. She'd come looking for me, so we ducked into that little stone shed."

"Rob didn't go with you?" the deputy asked. They both shook their heads, but he caught her sneaking a look at Emery. "You stayed where you were, didn't go looking for Rob and Tammy?" He saw Whitney and Emery share a glance, both looking suspicious. "I can tell that there is more to the story. I need the truth."

Emery sighed. "Whit was panicked about her friend. I tried to get her to stay where it was safe, but she took off."

"You didn't go after her?" Jaden asked.

"I'd had so much to drink," Emery said in his defense, "I was having a hard enough time just standing up, and then all hell broke loose."

The deputy wasn't through with these three, but he figured whatever they were hiding would come out eventually. He'd been waiting impatiently for news on Olivia Brooks and was becoming more anxious by the minute when his cell phone rang. He saw it was the head of the search and rescue party and quickly picked up, afraid the news wasn't going to be good.

"We found Rob Perkins. I think you'd better come take a look. It appears his death wasn't accidental."

"I'll be right there," Jaden said, taken aback. What had been going on out here even before the tornado?

Chapter Four

Jaden shone his flashlight beam on the body crushed under the old block wall before calling for backup to secure the scene where Rob Perkins had been killed. He'd seen at once what the rescue crew had. Deep footprints in the dirt, where it appeared someone had stood—and waited?—before struggling to push a portion of the wall over his victim—who hadn't been dead very long. The deep tracks in the soil were a dead giveaway this hadn't been an accident.

Perkins lay on his back, his body crushed under the blocks and cement. Only his head and shoulders were free, his arms raised as if he'd been trying to ward off what was coming for him.

At the sound of a bloodcurdling scream from higher up on the hillside, Jaden felt his heart drop. Wasn't that the area where Emery had told him Olivia had gone with Cody?

He turned to the state law-enforcement officer who'd arrived. "If you keep everyone away from here until the rest of the state Department of Criminal Investigation arrive, I'll see to whatever that is," he said and took off up the hill. It was hard getting around in the debris. He'd had to make a wide circle to get to the small crowd on the hillside.

As he drew closer, he saw several people standing over a hole in the ground. Behind Jaden, the sun was starting to rise over the mountains, turning the sky pink. One of the two rescue workers was attempting to climb down into the hole with the help of the other. The woman was standing off to the side. Olivia?

"What's going on?" the deputy called to them.

"We have an injured man down in an old root cellar," he called back as Jaden advanced on them.

As the woman turned, Jaden felt a start. Relief made his knees go weak. It was Olivia and she didn't seem to be injured. She seemed startled to see him.

"I hadn't heard that you were back in Montana," he said as he glanced in the hole. He'd gotten only a glimpse of Cody Ryan lying awkwardly in the bottom of what was left of the root cellar. He appeared to be unconscious.

As he felt the ground shift under him, he quickly stepped back. Taking Olivia's arm, he drew her away from the hole as the search and rescue team did their work.

Living in Fortune Creek to the north, he'd only recently met Cody. He was the high school sweetheart she'd told him about. After what Cody had told him about how she'd broken his heart, he hadn't expected to hear that they'd been together out here.

"He was fine when I left him," she kept saying now.

"He wasn't injured in the storm?" Jaden asked.

"No, he was fine. He couldn't climb out. I told him I would go get help, but when I came back…" She began to cry. "I don't understand what could have happened. And…" She motioned to a spot along the wall away from Cody's body. "We found those bones. Cody said they're human."

The deputy shone his light on the bones. Cody might be right, he thought. They appeared to be human bones. They'd know more once the coroner had a look at them. His mind was more on what Olivia was doing out there, of all places, with her old boyfriend. Not that it was any of his business. Not anymore.

Jaden had agreed with Cody on their chance encounter that Olivia was indeed a heartbreaker.

With a sigh, he pushed that thought away. He already had one suspicious death. Now this. "You climbed out and went for help?" He couldn't help but wonder why it had taken her so long. "How long ago was that?"

"I don't know. I got turned around trying to navigate this mess out here." She sounded close to tears. The debris had made it difficult to move. Look how long it had taken him to make it up the hill. But he couldn't wrap his mind around what Olivia was doing with Cody out here, in the middle of nowhere, in the middle of the night. If Cody had been injured after she'd left him, could it have been the same person who'd pushed a wall over on Rob Perkins? Where was Olivia when that was happening?

One member of the search and rescue team, a paramedic, confirmed that Cody's vitals were strong. His only injury appeared to be a blow to the head.

"Deputy," he called up. "There's a rock down here with his blood on it. Would you like me to bag it for you?"

"Please," Jaden said and saw Olivia shoot him a look.

"You think someone did this to him on purpose?" She seemed shocked at even the idea.

"Did you see anyone else around before you left Cody?" he asked, telling himself whatever his problems were with Olivia, she wasn't a killer.

"No, it was dark, and all I could think about was getting him help out of that hole."

"But you're sure he wasn't injured when you left him?"

"He was fine," she repeated more adamantly. "He just

couldn't get out. He insisted I go get help." She started to cry. "If I'd stayed—"

"You might have been injured as well," he told her. "Do you know anyone who might have wanted to harm him?"

She shook her head. "No. That is, I don't know. I've been gone all these years."

Exactly, he thought. "How long have you been back?"

"Only a few days."

Jaden nodded. "You and Cody together again?" He knew she and Cody had been close from the time they were kids. They'd grown up next door to each other and had years of history.

She seemed surprised by the question. "No."

"But you were out here with him." He hated that he sounded like a jealous lover. He needed her to tell him why, after being gone for years, she was here with her old boyfriend at what was now a murder scene. A double murder scene, if Cody didn't make it. And they still had people missing.

"We're just friends." She shook her head. "After tonight, maybe not even that anymore."

He felt his pulse jump at her words. "Did the two of you have an argument?"

She seemed to realize what he was asking. "I didn't do anything to him," she snapped indignantly. "I told you he was fine when I left."

At the sound of more sirens headed their way, Jaden stepped away to make two calls. One to the coroner, the other to the EMTs to tell them that they were needed high on the hillside to help get an unconscious man out of a root cellar.

Disconnecting, he stepped back over to where Olivia

was standing, hugging herself. Her face was streaked with dirt and tears. Still, she looked beautiful.

His cell rang. He stepped away to talk to the state crime team. Photographs of the scene had been taken and they were ready to get the body to the morgue. A helicopter had been arranged to airlift Cody Ryan to the hospital. One of their biggest problems was moving through all the wreckage left by the tornado.

Jaden kept looking back at Olivia, standing alone as a team worked to maneuver Cody out of the hole. There was still some speculation about where the helicopter would be able to land. At least the sky was getting lighter, visibility better.

He caught a glimpse of Cody and his head wound as he was brought up. Clearly, it had bled a lot, as head wounds tended to do. The rock he'd been hit with was large. Too large for the average person to throw down into a hole onto a man. But it could have been rolled. Not that Jaden had noticed any rocks like it nearby, none especially in the hole, except for the one that had injured Cody Ryan.

Jaden couldn't believe he had one suspicious death on his hands and an assault, along with two missing people: Jenny Lee and Dean Marsh.

As Olivia watched an unconscious Cody Ryan being lifted from the hole in the ground, Jaden observed her. He didn't want to believe she'd had anything to do with what had happened out here tonight. But he couldn't stop questioning what she'd been doing there with Cody to begin with.

More rescuers arrived to help dig through the debris for bodies as the sun rose behind the mountains, announcing the new day. The deputy took statements from everyone, let the parents of Tammy and Whitney take their daughters home, and then made calls to both Jenny Lee's husband and Dean Marsh's wife.

To his surprise, Jenny was home, her husband said. She'd called him to pick her up. From the emotion he heard in the husband's voice, he was aware that Jenny had been out in Starling with Dean Marsh.

"Did you happen to see anyone else when you picked up your wife?"

"You mean someone like Dean Marsh?" Tom Lee asked sarcastically. "No. I didn't see him."

Jaden asked to speak to Jenny, who sounded contrite. She swore that she and Dean had gotten into an argument and she'd taken off, walking down the road, where she'd called her husband and he'd come to pick her up. They'd just missed being caught in the tornado.

The deputy thanked her and kept the rescue workers searching for Dean Marsh's body as the new day began. He called his boss, Sheriff Brandt Parker, to let him know that he had one suspicious death, another man unconscious with a suspicious injury, and a missing man who'd been involved with another man's wife.

"That's all?" Brandt said.

"No. The storm uncovered some human remains. Oh, and my former fiancée is here with the unconscious man who is being transported to the hospital."

His boss swore. "And I thought I had a rough night with all the storm calls. Any suspects?"

"Lots of them, including Elden Rusk's ghost. I wouldn't be surprised if they all tell me they saw Rusk in the storm, walking away from Starling, carrying something heavy."

"The gold," Brandt joked. "What the devil were they doing out there?"

Good question, he thought. "Some kind of Halloween

dare, apparently. Though one of them could have had an ulterior plan to commit murder. The confusion during the tornado gave him or her the perfect opportunity." He shuddered as the sun rose so he could see the devastation and how little was left of Starling. "It's a miracle any of them survived."

"Let alone Rusk." For Jaden, Rusk was no laughing matter. He was the boogeyman who'd come out of his closet at night all during his childhood. "Good luck narrowing down the suspects."

"The coroner says there are two sets of human remains. One a teenage girl and the other a man somewhere between twenty-five and thirty. Apparently, they were buried together in the root cellar."

"All in a night's work," the sheriff said. "I'm finishing a case up here or I would help you."

"I'm good," Jaden said, then thought of Olivia. Not as good as he was pretending to be. What was she doing back here, let alone with Cody Ryan?

THE MORNING WAS almost gone by the time Olivia walked into her mother's house. She'd gotten a ride into town with one of the rescue team after giving her statement to Jaden. Just her luck that she'd been in Starling with her former high school boyfriend and the investigating deputy had been her former fiancé.

"You're not planning to leave town, are you?" he'd asked her. "I need you to stick around because the state boys might want to talk to you about what happened out in Starling."

"I'm not going anywhere."

"You staying out at the house with your mother?"

"I am."

He'd been all business, all sheriff's deputy, not the man she'd almost married, so she'd done her best to do the same. She'd imagined seeing him again but never under these circumstances. She wished that she'd called him as soon as she'd returned. She'd definitely thought about it. But after the way they'd left things when the engagement had ended, she wasn't sure he'd want to talk to her—let alone care that she was back in the area.

"Jaden?" It was the first time she'd said his name in so long, it had sounded strange on her lips. "Was Rob really murdered?" He'd nodded. "They still haven't found Dean?" He'd only shaken his head. "You can't really believe that I had anything to do with what happened out here. That I did something to Cody."

"Like leave your former boyfriend to die in that hole after clobbering him with a rock? Someone killed Rob and I suspect someone attacked Cody. The same person could have done something to Dean Marsh as well. Or had help with all three."

She had felt her eyes widen, alarmed that he would even say something like that. "You know me," she'd cried. "You know I had nothing to do with any of it."

His answer had been evasive. "The investigation is ongoing." He'd sounded so cold, not that she could blame him. He'd even asked her about the last time she'd seen Rob Perkins. If she hadn't gotten turned around after leaving Cody in the root cellar, it wouldn't have made her look so guilty. It had been dark and there'd been so much debris to try to get through… But she'd said all of that to him and it appeared he hadn't believed anything she'd told him. What he must think of her.

He'd asked if she'd seen anyone after she and Cody had gone for a walk. "I only saw them from a distance when I heard the girls with Emery and Rob screaming. I glimpsed them down by the creek playing around. After that I never saw any of them again." She'd registered his expression and felt her ire rise. "*You know me.* You know I'm not a killer." He hadn't commented. "I can't believe this."

"Let's get you a ride home" was all he'd said after that.

HER MOTHER WAS pouring herself a cup of coffee as Olivia came into the kitchen. "You've been out all night?" Then Sharon Brooks took a good look at her. "What happened to you?" she demanded, alarmed.

"I got caught in a tornado." She poured herself a cup of coffee, even though the smell made her stomach roil. Cupping the mug of hot coffee in her hands, she tried to quit shaking. "I almost died. Cody…" Her voice broke and she couldn't continue.

"Cody Ryan? You were with him? I thought that was over a long time ago?"

Olivia shook her head, too exhausted to explain why she'd gone out with him tonight, let alone everything that had happened. She kept seeing Cody down in the root cellar, bleeding and unconscious. If that wasn't awful enough, she couldn't forget Deputy Jaden Montgomery's expression when he'd questioned her. He actually believed she could be responsible for what had happened to Cody, let alone the others?

"I should never have come home."

"Why did you after six years without hardly a word?"

She looked at her mother and felt a wave of guilt. Cody was right. She hadn't looked back when she'd left, not even to do more than occasionally keep in touch with her mother. But if anyone should be able to understand why she'd left, it was her mother.

Sharon had left small-town Montana, only to return home

after she'd realized she was pregnant with Olivia. She'd moved in with her parents. Her mother and her grandparents, to make ends meet, had both raised Olivia. After her grandfather had died, Olivia had gone off to college, but her mother had stayed to take care of her own mother until her death.

Olivia took a sip of her coffee. "You came back here because you had no place to go," she said. "I came home for the same reason."

"You're pregnant?"

She shook her head. How could she explain that her dream hadn't turned out the way she'd thought it would? She'd gotten her degree in business administration and had no trouble getting a job. But she hadn't been able to explain the hollowness she had felt. She'd been haunted by the feelings that she'd made the wrong choices and not just with her job. She'd felt as if she'd left something undone back here and that she'd needed to go home.

"Don't you think I know why you fell in with Cody Ryan and then broke his heart when you hightailed it out of here? You didn't want to be me."

"Mom—"

"It's all right. I don't blame you. I never resented it. You had to leave. I wish you had at least come home once in a while to see me, but I understand that too. What I don't understand is why you came back now. I suppose you know that Jaden Montgomery is now a deputy over in Fortune Creek. Is it true what I heard, that the two of you were engaged?"

Olivia waved that away, definitely not wanting to talk about her broken engagement. "I saw him last night. He's in charge of the investigation out in Starling, where the tornado hit, almost destroying the entire community. Rob

Perkins is dead, Cody's unconscious and Dean Marsh is missing."

Her mother shook her head. "I won't even ask what you were doing out there." Her expression softened as she asked, "Are you still in love with one of these men? Is that what brought you back?"

Olivia felt tears blur her vision as she shrugged. Maybe she was only in love with the past and that feeling of being silly and a fool in love with her whole life ahead of her. "I missed them both in their own ways."

Her mother rolled her eyes and rose to pour herself more coffee. "Your grandmother was right about you. She always said you were too much like me, just give your heart away willy-nilly. Go get a shower and go to bed. You look like you're going to fall on your face. I'll make you some breakfast later."

She kissed her mother on the cheek and headed for the bathroom, knowing it was going to take more than a shower and sleep to make this nightmare go away.

Chapter Five

Jenny Lee finally opened the door after the deputy had pounded on it, repeatedly calling out, "Sheriff's Department." He knew she was inside, curtains drawn, car in the drive. When she did finally answer, she only opened the door a crack, so she could peer out.

"I need to speak with you, Mrs. Lee," Jaden said. He could see only one of her eyes from where she hid behind the open door. It was red and swollen. He'd waited until her husband had left for work, needing to speak with her alone. "We can talk here or I can take you down to the sheriff's office, if you prefer, as part of my murder and assault investigation."

"I don't know anything," she cried. "Can't you just leave me alone?"

"I'm sorry, but I can't."

She didn't move for a moment, then finally pushed open the door to let him in as she turned and retreated into the house. As soon as he entered, he saw that there had been a struggle. A coffee table was splintered in one corner, broken glass from what appeared to be a lamp glittered on the worn wood floor, and he could see a shattered mirror over the fireplace.

He swore under his breath as he closed the door behind

him and followed her to the rear of the house. It wasn't until she turned that he saw her black eye. She was a petite young woman with shoulder-length dark hair and a cowed expression, as if she'd had a rough life. "If you'd like to file charges against your husband—"

"No," she said with an adamant shake of her head. "I'm fine."

He could have argued that, given the painful way she was moving. He'd seen enough women like her to know her situation would only get worse if she stayed. But he knew she wouldn't want to hear it.

"Let's go out on the back porch," Jenny said. "I haven't felt like cleaning up yet. Watch where you step."

Gingerly he worked his way through the broken glass. Once on what was a closed-in sun porch, she sat down, pulling her legs up under her. She wore a sweat-suit set, the long-sleeved top smeared with blood.

Jaden still hadn't learned how to deal with domestic disputes. It was obvious that Tom Lee had physically abused his spouse. Jaden's first instinct was to go to Tom Lee's work and drag him outside. But unless Jenny filed charges…

"I need to get a statement from you about what happened last night in Starling," he said, pulling out his notebook. "You were there with Dean Marsh?" She nodded. "How long have the two of you been seeing each other?"

"For a while," she said.

"Weeks? Months?"

"I don't see what that has to do with—"

"Dean is missing, presumed dead. With one man murdered and another assaulted and in a coma, I need to know what was going on last night in Starling besides a tornado."

"You think Dean's dead?" There was a catch in her voice.

Her eyes filled with tears for a moment before she bit her lip and made a swipe at them. "We'd been meeting secretly for a few months."

"Were you with him when the tornado hit?" Jaden asked.

She shook her head. "We'd had an argument. I left and walked up the road. When I saw the storm coming, I called my husband to come get me."

"What did you argue about?" he asked.

Jenny gave him an impatient look. "Dean wanted me to leave my husband so we could be together. He was going to tell his wife."

"You refused?"

"I realized we'd both been kidding ourselves. Neither of us could leave our spouses. It's financial suicide and that's if they didn't kill us. I'd realized that it had to stop or it might cost me my marriage."

"You told him you were going to tell your husband?"

She nodded. "He got really angry, accusing me of leading him on, and bringing up things from our past. He said I would destroy both of our marriages, and for what? We wouldn't be together and our spouses would put us through hell. I told him I didn't care—that it was over. I got out of the truck and walked away to call my husband to come get me."

"What did Dean do?"

"I don't know. I didn't look back. All I could think about was getting home." She looked down at her hands, picking at something under her fingernail.

"Are you regretting that now?" He'd had to ask.

She slowly lifted her head, determination a brittle gleam in her gaze. "I love my husband. This is all my fault."

He wanted to tell her that most abused wives blamed themselves—even those who hadn't had an affair with another man. That her husband had no right to beat her, no matter how upset he was. But Jaden saved his breath. He'd send over a rep from a local counseling agency. Hopefully, someone would be able to give Jenny some perspective.

"Where was your husband last night after the storm, after you came home?" he asked.

"Here with me."

"All night?"

She nodded, almost daring him to argue differently.

"You'll testify under oath to that, knowing what happens if you perjure yourself?" he asked.

"Yes."

The deputy put his notebook and pen away and rose. "If you change your mind about filing charges against your husband—"

"I won't."

"If you think of anything else that can help us find Dean Marsh, or if you hear from him, please give me a call at the Fortune Creek sheriff's office."

With that, he tipped his Stetson and made his way to his patrol SUV, telling himself all he could do was his job, but sometimes it was very difficult when he couldn't save those most vulnerable who needed saving.

OLIVIA HAD TRIED to sleep but couldn't. She kept thinking of Cody and wishing she'd never agreed to go with him to Starling. Now he might die. She'd never forgive herself for leaving him alone down in that hole. She had no idea who might have attacked him after she'd gone for help. The whole night had been a nightmare. She couldn't believe that Rob was dead, murdered, Cody unconscious in the hospital and Dean missing. How was that possible?

At a tap on her bedroom door, she looked up from where she'd been trying to sleep to see her mother in the doorway.

"The deputy is here to see you." The deputy. Jaden.

Her pulse kicked up a beat at the thought of seeing him again. He'd been just doing his job last night, but he'd been so distant. It had hurt her heart. She took a breath and let it out. "Tell him I'll be right out." As her mother closed the door, Olivia rose. She had showered and changed clothes after returning home earlier. Still, she went into the bathroom to brush her teeth and at least run a comb through her hair.

She stared at her face in the mirror for a few moments, surprised by the dark circles under her eyes, the paleness of her skin. Her injuries were all minor, including the cuts and bruises on her face and hands, but she felt weak from the shock of everything that had happened.

How could she not feel lucky to be alive? But the thought brought her no comfort. Cody was in the hospital, possibly fighting for his life, Rob was dead, and who knew what had happened to Dean.

And now she was being forced to confront her past. The decisions she'd made, the pain she'd caused. What choice did she have with Jaden being the deputy in charge of the investigation? There was too much history between them. Last night, he'd asked if she and Cody were together. How could she explain that she'd felt comfortable with him because he was familiar? That he'd felt safe. That she'd missed that closeness they'd once shared. He'd been a friend from a less confusing time.

What she hadn't considered was that Cody might have a different memory of their time together, especially of how it had ended. What if he never regained consciousness? Or what if, she realized with a start, he did wake up and he thought she was the one who'd attacked him?

But the real question was why she hadn't contacted Jaden when she'd returned home, knowing he was close by in Fortune Creek and a deputy sheriff now. Because she hadn't thought he'd want to hear from her. Still, wasn't he the real reason she'd come home? It was more complicated than that, she thought. Much more complicated.

Olivia found him waiting for her in the living room. Her mother had made coffee and poured him a cup. Both seemed nervous. "Is this about Cody? Is he…?" She couldn't bring herself to say the words.

"He hasn't regained consciousness yet, but he's still alive," the deputy said. "I just needed to ask you a few more questions about last night. If you have a minute?" He glanced past her. "If you don't mind, Mrs. Brooks…"

Her mother seemed a little surprised but acquiesced. "Then I'll leave you two to it," she said, then looked to Olivia. "If at any point you feel the need, you can call our family lawyer."

She waved her away with "I'm fine." Once her mother was gone, she stayed standing, unsure where to sit or what to say. "I don't need a lawyer, do I?"

"That would be up to you."

She shook her head. "You know I didn't harm anyone last night." When he said nothing, she felt as if she might cry. "You *know* me."

EARLIER, JADEN HAD been sitting across from Sharon Brooks, turning the brim of his Stetson nervously in his fingers, when Olivia had finally come out of her bedroom.

He'd risen to his feet, his gaze taking in the lack of color in her face, the cuts and bruises, the dark circles around her eyes. She'd appeared exhausted, hurt and scared. He'd been struck by how vulnerable she looked. His heart had gone out to her.

For a moment, she was his Livie, the woman he'd fallen head over heels in love with. He wanted to pull her into his arms and assure her that everything was going to be all right. But he couldn't promise that since he wasn't sure he knew this woman as well as he'd once thought.

Did he really believe she'd had anything to do with what had happened last night in Starling? He'd known Livie intimately back in college. But when she'd gotten her dream job after graduation and talked about postponing the wedding indefinitely, he'd been shocked. No way had he seen it coming.

She was the woman he'd been ready to marry right after graduation. Heck, by now they could have a child or two. The thought hurt his chest. He'd been looking forward to marriage, kids, their own house. Worse, he'd been ready to follow her anywhere her career took her—even if it meant leaving Montana.

After the breakup, he'd taken the job in Fortune Creek. He'd found he loved being a deputy, helping people, putting away the bad ones. It wasn't perfect, but then, it was such a detour from the life he'd had planned with Livie, it felt right.

Seeing her again had knocked him off-kilter. He hadn't expected her to come back to Montana—let alone here, so close to Fortune Creek and him. And now she was mixed up dead center in his investigation.

Determined to keep this official and not dig through the past, he pulled out his notebook. "Tell me again how you ended up in Starling."

Olivia blinked as if she hadn't expected him to ask about the investigation.

"Nice to see you, too, Jaden. Yes, I'm glad to be home.

No, I wish I hadn't run into old high school friends and decided to go with them out to Starling on Halloween." She took a seat in the chair her mother had vacated across from the couch. Jaden sat back down in the same spot on the couch where he'd been earlier and took out his pen, warning himself to keep this professional.

"So how long had you been back when this was planned?" he asked, not looking at her.

"A couple of days. It wasn't planned. It was just spur-of-the-moment."

He shook his head. "I don't think so. Whoever wanted to kill Rob, possibly Cody and Dean, too, planned this. It might have seemed spur-of-the-moment to you, but someone was behind this."

She stared at him in obvious shock. "No, I can't believe that."

"You think it was just old friends getting together where possibly three of them might have ended up dead?"

She stood up and began to pace. "It wasn't like that. We had a couple of beers. We were reminiscing, laughing and having fun together."

"Who suggested it?" he asked, and she frowned.

"Emery. Or maybe it was Rob. I don't remember."

"You sure it wasn't Cody?" She shook her head. "How was it that you and Cody ended up at Starling?"

"He asked if I wanted to go. At the time, it sounded like fun. I didn't know everyone was going to pair off and disappear or I never would have gone."

"Tell me again who all was at the bar," Jaden said, his eyes on his notebook.

"Cody, Emery, Rob and Dean," she said.

He looked up at her then. "They weren't with dates or their wives or girlfriends at the bar that night?"

"It wasn't that unusual in the old days," she said, sounding defensive. "I used to hang out with them, play pool, go fishing. We were all just friends."

"Just you and the boys, huh?"

Her eyes narrowed with anger. "I told you about them when you and I were in college. They were old friends. That's why I agreed to go that night. I thought…" She shook her head. "It turned out to be a mistake even before the tornado."

"A mistake?"

"Cody still resents me leaving. He feels trapped here and…" She waved a hand through the air. "They're his issues, but me getting to leave is a bone of contention between us. Why is my relationship with him so important to you?" she demanded with obvious irritation.

"So you did argue."

She groaned. "Do we have to do this, Jaden?" Their gazes met. "You know I didn't attack Cody."

He wished he did. If she had rolled a rock down into that hole, she might not have realized it would hit him in the head and knock him unconscious. It could have been impulsive, like ending an engagement without any warning.

"Describe for me again what happened that night."

He listened as she told the same story she had last night. She'd left Cody to get help. He'd been fine.

"Any idea who might have wanted to harm him?" She shook her head again. "What about Rob or Dean?" Another shake of her head.

"I've been gone, remember?"

"I remember." He held her gaze for a long moment. They didn't have anything to say to each other, but there'd once been a time when they used to talk for hours. He had often called her at night, lying in bed. He'd loved the sleepy sound of her voice and had imagined her lying there.

But that was back when they'd been engaged. Back when he'd thought that one day she would be lying in bed next to him, talking about their day or their kids or their new dreams, shared dreams.

"Tell me where everyone else was when you and Cody left the group to wander up the hillside."

With a sigh, she repeated everything she'd told him before.

"Cody and I were fine. He saved my life when the house above us was ripped away in the tornado."

"Must have been terrifying." He couldn't imagine what she'd been through, but Livie had always been strong.

"It was. Then the tornado moved on. We saw the bones that had been dislodged from the soil. The ladder had been ripped away, but Cody helped me climb up the shelves. Unfortunately, they barely held my weight, so he couldn't use them to get out. I didn't want to leave him down there, but he insisted I go for help."

"That's the last time you saw him conscious?"

"I still don't understand what could have happened." She shook her head. "When I came back, he was lying down there motionless."

"Had you seen any rocks down there? Any that could have dislodged and struck him?"

She straightened her shoulders. "Like you said, I was terrified. I wasn't really looking around. But I think it was just dirt. That's why Cody was worried about it caving in more." She met his gaze. "You think someone purposely tried to hurt him?"

"Who of your group would want to do that?" Jaden asked.

"No one. They were his friends."

"Including Rob Perkins? There wasn't anything going on between them…? Any disagreements?" He saw her hesitate. "What?"

"Cody wasn't happy with Dean for bringing Jenny. He thought it was going to lead to trouble since they were married to other people."

"And Cody is close with Rob and Emery?" he asked.

Again, she hesitated. "I got the impression that Rob and Emery haven't matured. They brought those girls, you know—they're out of high school, but not old enough to drink."

Jaden thought the whole bunch of them were trying too hard to bring back their high school days. They appeared to be holding on to a past that was long gone. But then again, he realized that he'd been holding on to thoughts of Olivia and the imagined day she might return to him.

And now here she was.

"You and Cody were together the entire time last night? Neither of you left the other until you got out and went for help?"

"Yes, we were together the entire time. When the storm hit, we climbed down in the root cellar. Cody locked the overhead door, but then the tornado ripped it away, leaving us stranded down there. If you're asking if either of us climbed out and killed Rob…" She shook her head. "Why would we?"

"Why would anyone want Rob dead?"

She seemed to think for a moment before glancing up. "Rob and Emery talked about finding the gold last night. Maybe he went looking for it. You're that sure his death wasn't an accident?"

Jaden nodded. "Was there anything that happened back in high school, an old grudge involving a girl maybe?"

"Not that I can recall. You should ask someone who's been here this whole time."

"I will." He closed his notebook. She hadn't changed her story. He didn't think he would get anything else out of her. Yet he hesitated. "So how long are you back for?"

"I don't know."

He hated that spark of hope that filled his chest like helium. He'd never gotten over her, and seeing her again had brought back all those memories and feelings. He reminded himself that Cody Ryan must have felt the same way. They'd both loved this woman and she'd left them both.

"Are you thinking about staying?" He'd strayed away from the investigation into dangerous territory and mentally kicked himself. But he couldn't help it. He had to know.

She met his gaze. "I'm not sure."

"What about your dream job?" He hadn't been able to help himself. "Never mind. It's none of my business." He rose, telling himself to leave it at that. The worse thing he could do was ask if there was a chance for the two of them. She'd made her feelings clear enough when she hadn't called to let him know she was back in town. Instead, she'd accepted a date with her old high school boyfriend.

He hated how pathetic he felt, but finding her in the area had left him off balance. It had been easier to tell himself she was gone and that he was fine when he couldn't see her. But with her back…

"If I have any more questions, I'll call," he said as he headed for the door. "Goodbye, Mrs. Brooks," he called, knowing she hadn't gone far.

"It's Sharon," she called back. "Since you were almost my son-in-law."

He felt his jaw tighten and glanced at Olivia. She looked

as uncomfortable as he felt. He gave her a nod, settled his Stetson on his head and left.

Once outside, he took a deep breath and let it out. He told himself to stick to his job. He had a killer to find. Maybe of more than one person, if Cody Ryan died. He turned his thoughts to Dean Marsh as he climbed into his patrol SUV and headed for the Marsh house.

Chapter Six

With her mother plying her with questions about what Jaden had wanted, about what had happened on Halloween out at Starling and about her plans for the future, Olivia couldn't take it anymore and left the house. She drove to the hospital, hoping for good news about Cody's condition.

Unfortunately, he was not able to have visitors. Deputy Jaden Montgomery had restricted all visitors to Cody's room, the head nurse told her, so she couldn't even see him—let alone find out his condition.

She was starting to leave when she looked down the hallway and saw a young woman come out of Cody's room. Slim, with blond, straight hair, wearing jeans and a T-shirt, the woman glanced toward the nurses' station. Olivia's gaze met hers. The woman quickly turned and took off in the other direction.

"I just saw someone come out of Cody Ryan's room," she hurriedly told the nurse.

"Are you sure it wasn't one of our nurses?"

"Yes. She was wearing jeans and a T-shirt, and when I saw her, she took off."

The head nurse rushed down the hall to check on the patient but quickly returned. Olivia wanted to admonish her for not keeping a closer eye on his room, but could see how upset the nurse was for letting it happen.

Leaving the hospital, Olivia glanced around, hoping to see the woman again as she drove down the main drag. She had no idea what she would do if she found the woman. But who she did see was Emery. He was just going into the bar where they'd all recently reunited.

Without questioning her intentions, she pulled into the first parking place she came to, got out and followed him. Jaden's questioning had more than bothered her. He'd gotten personal at the end and she'd seen how much it had upset him. He'd been trying so hard to keep it professional.

He'd left her feeling as if maybe he did still care. That gave her hope. If it wasn't for this investigation… That, she told herself, was why she was headed into the bar to see Emery. This wouldn't end until whoever had killed Rob and attacked Cody was found and arrested. And, like she'd told Jaden, she'd been away too long and didn't know what had been going on in her absence.

That first night in the bar, it had felt like old times. But by the time they'd reached Starling, she'd sensed that it wasn't—and not just for her and Cody. The old gang wasn't as close as they'd been. Still, she couldn't believe that one of them was a murderer.

Stepping into the dimly lit bar, she had to give her eyes a moment to adjust before she spotted Emery. He had taken a stool at the bar some distance from anyone else. He had a drink in front of him, even though it was still morning. All his attention seemed to be on his drink, as if he could find answers in the glass in front of him.

As she approached, she wondered if he was meeting someone. She'd never been as close with Emery as she had been with the others back in high school. He was the bad boy, the biker, the kid who'd lived, so to speak, on the wrong side of the tracks. Even in small towns without railroad tracks, there was sometimes a part of town less desirable.

"Is this stool taken?" she asked as she started to join him.

He seemed surprised to see her but smiled and appeared glad for the company. "Have a seat. What are you drinking?"

"I'd take a cola."

He laughed. "Teetotaler," he joked and signaled the bartender. Like her, he had scrapes and bruises but had miraculously survived the tornado, as had the two young women with him and Rob. "You been over to the hospital?"

She nodded. "They wouldn't tell me anything about his condition or let me see him."

He gave a shake of his head. "I heard he's still unconscious. My aunt knows someone who works there. I can't believe what happened."

Olivia wasn't sure if he was talking about Rob's murder, Cody's injury, Dean's disappearance or the tornado. "I know what you mean," she said as the bartender put a napkin and her drink in front of her. She thanked him and turned to Emery. "What happened after I left town?"

He frowned. "What do you mean?"

"The old gang. I picked up on what I thought was good-natured jabs that first night at the bar, so I didn't think too much about it. Rob was leaving town, going to his dream job. Now I realize that not everyone was happy for him."

"I was. Why wouldn't I be?" Emery said almost irritably as he reached for his glass. He drained it and signaled the bartender for another.

"I know you and Rob have been best friends almost

since you were born. At least, you were best friends when I left. Did that change?"

"Why are you asking me these questions?" He eyed her suspiciously.

"I'm just trying to understand what might have changed since I left."

He sighed. "A lot changes in six years." The bartender took his empty and left a fresh drink, but Emery didn't pick it up right away. He seemed lost in thought.

Olivia took a sip of her soft drink and waited.

"Rob and I weren't as tight as we used to be, maybe." He shrugged. "That's why I was excited about going out to Starling on Halloween. We hadn't done anything like that in a very long time. As for the old gang… We're not in high school anymore. We all have jobs, responsibilities."

She definitely knew that feeling of a job becoming her entire life. She'd thought it would make her happy. She was making money, and she had her own place, though it was small and the neighbors noisy, and the hours at work long. She'd woken up one morning to realize she wanted more.

Emery looked down the bar for a moment before he said, "A lot of our friends left, greener grass, like I have to tell you. It's not like only the losers stay." He picked up his drink and took a gulp, his eyes on the back bar.

"Have you ever thought about leaving?"

He shook his head. "I left for a while after you did. Just got on my bike and checked out other places." He smiled over at her. "I found out that there is no place like Montana, and I hightailed it back. You're thinking that whoever killed Rob was jealous he was getting out of here and they weren't?" His expression said he didn't believe that was the case.

She was reminded that it was Rob who had wanted to go

out to Starling and stay until midnight. If he'd been worried that one of the others resented his success, he certainly hadn't shown it. "Do you really believe there is gold still hidden out in Starling?"

Emery chuckled. "Doubtful. But it's like the other legends about the place. It gives people something to talk about, dream about."

"What would you do if you found the gold?" she asked and took another swallow.

"Depends on how much is there."

She smiled over at him. "Enough to take a trip around the world."

"That's just it. I wouldn't go anywhere. I'd buy me a place on the lake. I wouldn't have to work, but I probably would. I'd stay right there." He laughed. "I guess I don't need any gold. I'm…content. Some people think that's just laziness talking, but I like my life. I wouldn't change it."

She studied him for a moment. "I understand completely." She told him about her dream job. "All those years of college and then the job…" She shook her head. "I realized it wasn't what I wanted." At the heart of it, she'd missed Montana, the familiar, the place she'd grown up in. Wasn't that why she'd come back? At least, that was what she'd told herself, not that she could deny Jaden had also been part of it. The problem was…even before Halloween night and what had happened, she'd held out little hope that Jaden would ever be able to forgive her for hurting him.

JADEN FOUND ANGIE MARSH loading suitcases into the back of her SUV as he drove up. The petite, slightly built brunette didn't look happy to see him as he got out of his patrol vehicle and walked toward her. "Going somewhere?" he asked, eyeing the suitcases. He saw that she had loaded numerous boxes in the back. None of it looked like anything of her missing husband's.

It had crossed his mind that she might be going to meet Dean somewhere, the two of them on the run together after Dean had killed Rob and almost succeeded in taking out Cody as well. What struck him was how much Jenny resembled Angie. Clearly, Dean had a type.

"I don't have time for this, Deputy," she said, pushing past him with a load in her arms. She wore jeans and a T-shirt with a band's name he'd never heard of. Her long dark hair was pulled up in a ponytail. But what really caught his eye was that she wasn't wearing her wedding ring.

On her way back to the house, he stopped her. "I just need a few minutes to talk to you about Dean." She hesitated, looking as if she'd prefer not to. "We can talk here or down at the sheriff's office."

With a sigh, she dusted off her jeans and motioned toward the house. "Let's make it quick. I don't want to be here when he comes back."

Did she really think he was coming back? She'd be in the minority, from what Jaden had heard around town. Pretty much everyone assumed he was on the run, either a murderer or just a philanderer. Some thought that Jenny Lee's husband, Tom, had probably found him that night and killed him. Why Dean's body hadn't turned up was anyone's guess.

The deputy followed Angie into the house, not surprised to see there were more items by the front door that she was apparently planning to load into her vehicle. She was clearing out, leaving not just her missing cheating husband, but town.

"You said you wanted to leave before Dean returned,"

Jaden said once she led him into the kitchen and pointed to a chair at the table after he declined coffee.

"Does that mean you've heard from your husband?"

She poured herself some orange juice, then turned her back to add something to it. When she sat down across the table from him, he could smell the vodka. "I haven't heard from Dean," she said. "I don't expect to."

"Why is that?"

Angie lifted a brow. "Wouldn't you be too ashamed to show your face in this town?"

"Because of what happened out in Starling on Halloween?" he asked, confused.

"We all know what happened. Dean was with that tramp, Jenny Lee."

"I thought maybe you were referring to Rob Perkins being killed and Cody Ryan being assaulted and in the hospital, still unconscious. You're that sure Dean didn't do it and that's why he's disappeared?" Jaden asked.

For a moment, she looked as confused as he was. Then she let out a bark of a laugh before picking up her drink. "Dean? A murderer?" She laughed some more before taking a large gulp of her juice. "Dean's a cheater, a liar and a ne'er-do-well who burns his bridges. Smell that?" she asked with a sniff. "That's a bridge burning. Clearly, you've never met my husband." She took another drink of her orange juice. "Dean's a lot of things, but a killer? No, he wouldn't have the stomach for it. He's gotten caught cheating and now he's afraid to come home and face the consequences."

Jaden told himself that maybe Angie was just a woman spurned who'd had enough and was cutting her losses. Yet he couldn't help feeling like there was more going on. "You're that sure he didn't have any conflicts with his two friends?"

"He was jealous of them, especially Rob, since he was leaving here to start a better life. But Emery?" She shook her head.

"I know you're angry with him, but there's a chance his body might still be found out in Starling," he warned. "The area is still being searched."

With a shake of her heard, she said, "Oh, he'll turn up, alive and well and lying through his teeth."

He felt himself studying her ring finger. There was only a ghost of a white line where it had been on her finger. He wondered if she hadn't taken it off sometime before all this.

"If you hear from him, please call me," he said as he rose to leave.

"Oh, I will. I'll want you to keep him away from me because I want him gone. I wish he was capable of murder. Then you could drive him to Deer Lodge to the state prison and we'd all be shed of him."

"One more thing," he said as if the thought had just come to him. "Where were you on Halloween night?"

She glared at him, then shook her head as if amused. "If I wanted to kill my husband, I wouldn't have driven all the way out to Starling in the middle of the night, Deputy. I would have just cut his throat while he slept next to me. Halloween wasn't the first time he was with Jenny Lee, by the way."

After leaving Angie, Jaden drove over to Whitney Clark's house and questioned her about Rob and Emery's whereabouts just before the tornado. He then stopped by her friend Tammy Bell's and got pretty much the same information from her.

Both had been scared and foggy on what had happened.

"Had Rob and Emery been arguing?" No.

"Had either been acting strangely?" To that, he'd gotten

confused looks. Clearly, neither girl had known either of them well enough to know. Both girls were grounded and still shocked and upset that they'd almost died.

As he was leaving the Bell residence, the hospital called. Cody had regained consciousness.

Chapter Seven

Cody felt himself falling in and out of sleep as he waited for the doctor to come back. Earlier, he'd told him that he had a severe concussion from a blow to the head. Cody had touched the bandage on his forehead, but he couldn't remember how he'd gotten it. His head hurt and he felt confused and anxious.

When the door opened, though, it was the deputy. He groaned silently, having learned that when a cop showed up, it was usually not a good sign.

"How are you feeling?" Jaden asked as if he really cared.

Cody doubted it since they'd been in love with the same woman. He wondered if the deputy had gotten over Olivia. He had his doubts.

The lawman dragged up a chair and, pulling out his notebook and pen, sat down. "Need to ask you some questions about Halloween night at Starling."

Cody frowned. He'd awakened in a hospital bed, wondering how he'd gotten there. "Halloween?" Why couldn't he remember? Actually, he was having trouble retrieving his last memory. "What is today?" Jaden told him. "I've lost three days?" He couldn't help being scared. He had no idea what had happened in those three days. They were now a dark hole.

The deputy studied him, no doubt thinking he was lying. But why would he need to lie? Why was the deputy here asking him questions unless something bad had happened?

"What do you remember?"

"Work." He frowned in concentration. "Friday, getting off work and going to the bar."

"And after that?"

Cody shook his head. "Nothing until I woke up in this bed. Are you going to tell me what happened?"

"I'd rather you remember on your own. The doctor said once the swelling goes down in your brain, you should remember more."

"Great," he said, leaning back in the bed. "You can't tell me how I got hurt?"

"There was a tornado."

"No kidding?"

"You probably don't recall who you were with or what you were doing in Starling."

Cody frowned. Of course he hadn't been alone. But a tornado? What had he been doing in Starling? "Sorry, nothing. I have no idea what I might have been doing out there."

"Let me know if you remember something," Jaden said as he saw the doctor coming down the hall. His time was up.

AFTER THE DEPUTY LEFT, Cody stared out the window, his heart pounding. He blamed his aching head for why he hadn't caught on sooner. Had someone tried to kill him? Why else was the law asking him all these questions? Something had happened at Starling. It had happened to him. He squeezed his eyes shut, grimacing at the pain as he tried to remember. For a moment, he thought he saw something on the edge of his memory, a fleeting image of a dark figure standing above him. But it was quickly gone. What scared him was that if he really was in danger, he wouldn't have any idea who he had to fear.

At a sound, his eyes flew open, startled to find someone right beside his bed, standing over him. "Krystal? What are you doing here?" he demanded, drawing back instinctively.

"Keep your voice down," she ordered. "I had to see you." She reached out to touch the bandage on his head.

He grabbed her hand. "You shouldn't be here. The deputy thinks someone tried to kill me."

She mugged a face at that and pulled up the chair close to the bed before sitting down. "Who'd want to kill you? That old girlfriend of yours. That's who you were with Halloween night, right?"

"Old girlfriend?" he asked, even more confused.

"Olivia Brooks," she snapped, no doubt thinking he was faking his confusion. "She's back in town. Why would you take her out to Starling?"

"I have no idea. I don't remember anything. I have a concussion."

She studied him with squinted suspicious eyes. "You don't know if she's the one who coldcocked you?"

"No." He frowned, making his headache worse. "I didn't even know she was back in town."

"You were with her at the bar the other night," Krystal snapped. "You're telling me you don't remember that either?"

He could understand why she was suspicious. "I guess it's a major concussion since I lost three days of memory. You didn't happen to be out there at Starling, did you?"

Krystal laughed at that. "Why would I want to hurt you? Whose idea was it for you and Olivia to go out there together?"

He groaned and pointed to his head. "You probably know more about it than I do."

"I know you cheated on me," she said and pulled a pout.

"We aren't together, so it's not cheating." He wished he'd rung for a nurse the moment he'd seen Krystal beside his bed. "I can't do this right now. I'm supposed to be resting."

She stood abruptly but stayed standing over him in a way that made him nervous. "Did you know that they didn't find Dean's body in the rubble left from the tornado? No one knows what happened to him."

Had someone mentioned a tornado? "Dean's missing?"

"Haven't they told you anything?" She sounded both surprised and delighted. "You know you were all out in Starling on Halloween night when the tornado hit, right?" She didn't give him time to answer. "Dean, Jenny, Emery, Rob and a couple of young girls. Then you don't know that Rob is dead. *Murdered.* Seems someone pushed a wall over on him." She made a pained face.

He felt as if she'd dropped an anvil on his chest. What the hell had happened out in Starling that night? "Rob was murdered?"

"Isn't that what I just said?"

He knew that Krystal had never liked Rob or Dean, especially since Jenny was married to Krystal's brother, Tom. "You sure you weren't out in Starling that night?"

Krystal smiled. "If I had been, then the head count would have been much higher. Olivia Brooks among the dead or wounded."

"Excuse me," a female voice said as the hospital room door opened. A nurse stood framed in the doorway. "Mr. Ryan needs his rest. Only family can visit."

"I'm his girlfriend," Krystal said, meeting his gaze as if daring him to argue otherwise.

"I'm sorry, but you'll have to leave," the nurse said.

Krystal kissed Cody on the mouth before turning to walk out the door.

"Are you all right?" the nurse asked him.

"Fine." It was a lie. He wouldn't be fine until he remembered everything about that night.

CODY WAS CONSCIOUS. Olivia felt weak with relief after the call from Emery with the news. She cared about her former best friend, boyfriend and neighbor. She'd been so afraid for him. She felt a second wave of relief. His being awake meant he could tell Jaden who had attacked him. Finally, she would be cleared of any wrongdoing.

Before she could rush to the hospital, the deputy called.

"Cody wants to see you. The nurse said you could see him for a few minutes because he is so insistent."

"I'll be right there," she said, anxious to find out what had happened after she'd left him to go for help.

Cody was propped up in bed, his head bandaged. He smiled as she walked into his hospital room, making her think they'd put any nastiness from Halloween night behind them. She realized he was staring at her as if just as relieved to see her as she was to see him. "Did Jaden tell you?"

"He said you wanted to see me. Did you tell him who attacked you?" she asked.

He started to shake his head but quickly stopped himself. His eyes closed for a moment. When he opened them, he was staring at her again. "I'm sorry. I thought Jaden would have… I can't remember *anything*. When I woke up, I didn't even remember you were in town, let alone that I'd apparently seen you at the bar. You're back in town?"

He sounded so surprised at that, but not half as surprised as she was to hear that he didn't remember anything from Starling. "Wait. You don't remember Starling, the tornado…?"

"Nothing. What were we doing out there? Were we together?"

She sat on the edge of the chair next to his bed. That was when she noticed the deputy standing in the doorway, watching them. "What did Jaden tell you?"

"Not much. He said he'd prefer that I remember on my own. But I heard there was a tornado that hit Starling and you were there with me?"

Olivia fought to swallow the lump that had formed in her throat. "It was just a bunch of old friends doing something foolish." She explained how Emery had come up with the idea at the bar the night before Halloween.

"We couldn't have known there would be a tornado," he said, frowning. "How was it that we survived?"

Before she could answer, the deputy stepped into the room. "That's enough for now," Jaden said. "I know you have a lot of questions. The doctor said you need to rest. Once the swelling goes down in your brain, you'll probably remember at least some of it."

Cody looked at Olivia. "Thanks for coming to see me."

She smiled and rose. "Just get well."

On the way down the hall toward the exit, Jaden stopped her.

"I couldn't let you tell him. I want him to remember on his own," the deputy said.

She couldn't hide her frustration. "I need him to remember so that I'm no longer a suspect." His expression didn't change. "You being angry with me isn't giving me confidence that I'm innocent until proven guilty. The way you're looking at me right now feels as if it's more about our broken engagement than what happened to Cody."

"How am I looking at you?"

"Like you want to see me behind bars," she snapped.

"Sorry, that's not my intention. I'm only trying to get to the truth."

"I've told you the truth." She shook her head, seeing that he still didn't believe her. "None of this has anything to do with me."

"Right. You were just an innocent bystander who just happened to be down in the root cellar alone with Cody. You wouldn't have hurt him," he said, studying her closely. "But aren't you at least curious to know who tried to kill your boyfriend?"

"He isn't my boyfriend," she declared. "We're just old friends."

"'The old gang.' Isn't that what you used to call them? I think you know more about them and what happened out there than you're telling me. They're still your friends."

Olivia wondered about that. Friends didn't kill each other. What was he asking? "They've had years together while I was gone. I hardly know them anymore."

"Right. You've been gone so long that none of this probably matters to you."

"That's not true." She had to look away. She knew what he was doing. "What is it you want from me?"

He looked down at his boots for a moment. "You know these people. They trust you. You're one of them." His gaze rose to meet hers and held it. "Someone's lying. If you hear something…"

"You want my help?" She hadn't meant to sound so shocked. With a sigh, she said, "I'm really not sure anyone will be telling me anything, but you have to know that I'll help any way I can." She started to turn away, but stopped.

"What did you find out about the bones we discovered in the root cellar?"

"They're checking dental records and DNA, but the coroner said the remains are those of a young girl of about sixteen."

"Is it Evangeline?"

He shrugged. "We'll see."

Olivia couldn't believe that he could doubt it. "Whose house was that root cellar in?" she asked, keeping him from walking away just yet.

Jaden hesitated. "My family's."

She felt her eyes widen in surprise.

"Please don't jump to conclusions. We left there before she disappeared. I don't know who moved into the house. Maybe no one."

"What about Elden Rusk?" she demanded. "Is he still alive? Could he have been in Starling that night?"

The deputy groaned. "If he's still alive, I really have my doubts he was in Starling on Halloween."

"Because you want it to be one of my old friends. Or better yet, me."

He shook his head. "Believe it or not, I'm just doing my job. I'll try to find Elden. I'll find out if he's been in the area." With that, he turned and headed down the hall to the nurses' station.

Olivia felt sick to her stomach as she watched him leave. What had she thought would happen when she came home? Certainly not this. Jaden was angry with her, which scared her. What if Cody remembered that they'd argued and thought she'd been the one to attack him down in the root cellar?

Glancing back down the hall, she saw the young woman she'd seen earlier exiting Cody's hospital room. She started to call down to the nurses' station to Jaden, but he was already gone and the head nurse was on the phone.

Turning toward Cody's room, she saw the blonde disappear around the corner. She went after her. As she passed a nurse, she alerted her that a patient in Room 9 needed help. Then she kept going after the blonde, determined to find out who she was.

By the time she reached the corner, the woman was halfway down the hallway. She called, "Excuse me! Could you please wait up?"

There was no way the woman hadn't heard. Quite the contrary. The blonde increased her speed.

Determined to find out who she was, Olivia ran after her. "I asked you to stop," she said when she drew closer.

The blonde said something rude and kept going.

Olivia grabbed her arm, spinning her around until they were face-to-face. "Who are you?" she demanded.

"Let go of me."

"Not until you tell me who you are and why you were in Cody's room."

The young woman's expression turned ugly. She jerked her arm free and, spitting out the words, said, "I have every right to see Cody. More right than you do. He's *my* boyfriend."

Olivia blinked. "Your boyfriend?" But before she could get more information, the blonde took off down the hall to the exit and was gone.

Staring after her, she realized that she should have known Cody would have been dating someone. He could have even been married after all this time. Cody Ryan had never gone long without a girlfriend—even back in grade school.

Chapter Eight

Jaden couldn't help being frustrated by this case, by everything. As he climbed into his patrol SUV, he admitted that seeing Olivia again had him so far off-kilter, he didn't know which way was up.

Worse, if she and Cody had argued the night of the tornado, which he suspected they had, she could have picked up a rock and flung it at him without thinking. While she'd never been impulsive, her decision to return home seemed that way. She didn't seem to have an answer for why she'd come home or how long she planned to stay. That wasn't like her.

After interviewing her, he'd checked. She'd quit her job, one that she'd worked so hard, apparently, to get since it was what she said she'd dreamed of since she was a girl. Why would she do that? He'd assumed she was happy with the decision she'd made after wanting to postpone their wedding indefinitely so she could fulfill that dream.

His cell phone rang. Pushing aside his suspicions and concerns about Olivia for the time being, he saw it was the crime lab.

"Thought you'd want to know about those bones uncovered up there," the technician said. "I'm not sure if you were informed, but there were two sets in that pile. The one set is from a teenage girl. The second set is male, somewhere from twenty-five to thirty."

"Will you be able to get DNA from them?" Jaden asked.

"Doubtful, but with the girl, quite a bit of her clothing had also been buried with her." Even before he described it, Jaden knew the bones were going to be Evangeline Rusk's.

"Were there any other remains, like a baby's?" No. That meant she hadn't been pregnant, the baby had been too small and its bones had deteriorated, or Evangeline had already given birth. Jaden thanked him and disconnected, thinking that he needed to find Elden Rusk, if he was still alive, and give him the news.

Meanwhile, he needed to talk to Emery Jordan. Starting his SUV, he headed for Emery's bike shop.

He found him working on what looked like a vintage Harley, all the parts spread out on the floor around him. Seeing the man at work, he was reminded of the expression "happier than a pig in mud."

Emery looked up, but it had taken Jaden yelling his name several times over the rock music playing in the garage area before he acknowledged him.

The deputy motioned toward the bike shop office and headed in that direction. Emery came in a few minutes later, wiping his greasy hands on a rag before he turned down the music. It was more tolerable in here than in the garage, but still loud.

"More questions?" Emery asked and took a seat behind a cluttered desk. "Have a seat."

Jaden pulled up a padded army-green chair from another era and sat. Emery had bought the old gas station furnished when he'd started his bike shop, the deputy recalled. "How's business?"

With a shrug, he said, "So-so. It will pick up. It's always

slow this time of year. Is that what you wanted to talk about, my business?"

"Actually, I wanted to talk about your relationship with Rob Perkins," Jaden said. "I understand Rob was an investor when you started the shop."

Emery's eyes narrowed. "You think I killed him so I wouldn't have to pay him back? He was the first person I paid back when I got the shop running."

"Okay, if not financial, did you two have any other kind of disagreement?"

"I know what you're looking for. An argument over a girl or a bet or jealousy because Rob was following his dream. Sorry, there was none of that. No girl, no bet, and I was happy for Rob. This," Emery said, indicating the bike shop, "has always been my dream. You're barking up the wrong tree. I would never have killed him or anyone else."

"What about Dean Marsh?"

"I don't have a gripe with him either. Did I approve of what he and Jenny were doing?" He shook his head. "None of my business."

"What about their spouses?" the deputy asked. "You involved with either of them?"

Emery laughed. "Involved? Me and Tom? Or me and Angie?"

"Either."

"Now you are just being silly."

"What about Rob and Dean or Rob and Cody? How'd they get along?"

The bike shop owner hesitated a little too long. "Fine, as far as I know."

Jaden studied him, picking up on something. Putting his notebook and pen away, he asked, "Why Starling? I heard it was your idea to go out there Halloween night."

"Really? I might have brought it up, but Rob's the one who suggested it to me. We'd gone out there before on Halloween growing up, so why not for old times' sake?"

Yes, why not? "Did anyone from your old group who was at the bar decide *not* to go?"

Emery thought for a moment before shaking his head.

"What about other people at the bar the night you all decided to do this?" the deputy asked. "Anyone in the crowd have a reason to be listening to your conversation? Anyone with a grudge against you or Rob or Cody or Dean?"

This time there was no mistaking it. Jaden knew he'd hit upon something. Emery looked away for a moment. "Krystal Lee. She and Rob used to date. They broke up when he started talking about a job on the West Coast. I remember seeing her at the bar that night. It was strange."

"Strange how?"

"She was with Jenny Lee. Neither of them drink alcohol. Jenny's in AA and Krystal's pregnant. I got the feeling that they were trolling, you know."

"So, they could have overheard your plans for Halloween?" Jaden asked.

Emery nodded. "They both left right after that, so maybe they heard what we were talking about."

"You said Krystal's pregnant? Is Rob the father of her baby?"

"He swears he's not." He seemed to realize what he'd said. "I guess it doesn't matter now."

Straightening his Stetson, Jaden rose. "Thanks. If you think of anything else…" He knew there was more; he could feel it.

He still had so many questions. Anyone with a grudge could have been at the bar that night, could have overheard the group's plans for Halloween—including Jenny and Krystal. He wondered how Jenny and Dean had ended up together at Starling that night, sans their spouses. His guess was that Jenny's husband's sister, Krystal, wouldn't have been all right with it.

But there was one way to find out. He'd ask Krystal.

As OLIVIA LEFT the hospital, she couldn't get the blonde off her mind. How could she not have realized Cody was in a relationship? A memory surfaced from that night at the bar. When she'd come up to the table, she recalled Dean elbowing Cody. She hadn't caught what he'd said. At the time, she'd thought Dean was kidding Cody because of his surprised look when he'd seen her.

Had anyone mentioned a girlfriend? The guys had all been there without dates or wives. But now that she thought about it, she knew Cody would have had a girlfriend. Back in their high school days, before they'd become serious, he'd never been without a date. He'd been like a magnet, always drawing the opposite sex to him. He might even have been serious about one or two of them. Like the blonde she'd seen at the hospital?

As she drove, something in the rearview mirror caught her eye. A dark-colored SUV behind her. She recalled it had pulled out behind her as she'd left the hospital parking lot. She hadn't thought anything of it, only noticing when she turned out of town—and it did as well.

She couldn't see the driver's face with the sun shining off the windshield, but she felt a prickle of concern as she sped up and the driver behind her did the same. Squinting in the mirror, she tried to read the dirty license plate on the SUV but couldn't make out the numbers and letters. Maybe it was someone she knew following her home.

Or not. Her instincts told her not. She started to reach

for her phone, only to stop herself. Was she really considering calling Jaden and telling him...what?

Slowing down, Olivia hoped the driver would pass her before they got very far out of town. Her mother's house was still a couple of miles up the road. It sat on five acres, with no other houses nearby, with no one around since Sharon had said she had a hair appointment in Eureka today.

The driver behind her slowed as well, even though there were no cars coming in the other lane, no reasons not to pass. Except for one.

Her heart began to pound. She gripped the steering wheel, trying to decide what to do. She wasn't about to try to outrun the driver. Why would anyone be following her?

Rob Perkins had been murdered and Cody attacked the other night at Starling. She'd been there. Was it possible the killer thought she'd seen something incriminating?

She flinched as she noticed in the mirror that the driver of the SUV came racing up behind her. Automatically, she hit the gas to keep him from crashing into the back of her. But when she looked up, she saw a deer standing next to the road.

Startled, the deer jumped forward onto the pavement. Olivia swerved away from it, but the driver behind her must not have seen it until it was too late. In her rearview mirror, she saw him also swerve and lose control as the deer bounded away and the SUV careened into the ditch. It came to a stop in the soft earth.

Olivia tried to catch her breath as she reached for her phone to call the deputy.

JADEN HAD HOPED to find Krystal Lee at home. He left a note for her on her door to call him when she returned and was heading for his patrol SUV when he got the call from Olivia.

The moment he heard her voice, he knew something had happened. "Slow down," he said, trying to assure her. "What happened?"

"Someone followed me after I left the hospital. I don't know if they were just trying to scare me or planned to run me off the road."

He listened as she described the dark-colored SUV and told him about the deer and the driver losing control and ending up in the ditch. "Where are you?"

"I'm at home. Mom's in town getting her hair done."

She was alone. He could hear the fear in her voice. "Stay there. I'm on my way."

The drive out of town didn't take long. He didn't bother with his lights and siren since there was so little traffic. Had it been summer with all the seasonal tourists, it would have been a different story. Still, he drove fast, worried about Olivia. The woman he knew didn't scare easily. But she'd been through a lot lately. He reminded himself that he still didn't know what had happened out at Starling to Rob Perkins. Or to Cody Ryan, for that matter, let alone Dean Marsh.

What he did know was that his former fiancée seemed to be dead center in the middle of it. If she was right about someone trying to run her off the road, her being back in town was becoming more dangerous for her.

He hadn't gone far when he saw the skid marks on the two-lane blacktop. Slowing, he saw the deep tracks in the earth at the edge of the road and even deeper tire tracks in the barrow pit. But the SUV had managed to drive out and was now gone.

Speeding up, he headed for the house Olivia had grown

up in with her single mother. She'd told him stories about her life there before he'd met her at college. She'd said she was afraid of becoming her mother—if she didn't get away from the small town and make something of herself.

He could relate. He'd also wanted to distance himself from his parents' life when he was younger. His parents had chased every alternative lifestyle before ending up living off the grid in Alaska. Fortunately, by then, he'd been on his own.

So, as determined as Olivia had been about getting away from here, what was she doing back? he asked himself as he pulled into the drive and she came running out.

Chapter Nine

When Jaden drove up in his patrol SUV, Olivia felt such a surge of relief that she ran out of the house and into his arms. Just seeing him had brought back such a rush of emotions after her earlier scare. As he closed his arms around her, she leaned into him, breathing in his familiar scent, soaking up his warmth and strength. She'd always felt so safe in his embrace.

He held her tight, his breath in her hair as he called her "Livie," his nickname for her. Just the sound of it was almost her undoing. She'd missed hearing it on his lips, missed the intimacy they'd shared, missed him.

"You're all right," he whispered. She was now—now that he was there. "It's okay."

She drew back to look into his handsome face and felt a pang of regret. How could she not miss what they'd had together? Worse, she could only blame herself that he was no longer in her life. When she'd heard that she'd gotten the job of her dreams, she'd thought only of postponing the wedding for a while. He was on his way to law school. She'd never considered he might want to go with her and, instead of postponing the wedding, would break off their engagement.

No wonder he'd thought she wasn't ready for marriage.

He released her now. Her heart fell as she saw the change in him. She ached with a longing she hadn't expected for him not to pull away. Wasn't this why she'd come home? She'd feared that she'd made the biggest mistake of her life by letting him go without putting up a fight for them. Now, as he went back to business, she feared it was too late. Cody had a girlfriend. What if Jaden did as well? She'd been such a fool.

Fighting tears, she tried to be as down-to-business as he was. "Did you find the SUV? Was the driver still there?" She felt bereft of his arms. Hugging herself, she looked down the road as if expecting the dark vehicle to appear.

"The driver was already out of the ditch," he said. "You happen to get a license plate number?" She shook her head. "How about a description of the vehicle?"

"A large, dark-colored SUV. Maybe a dark gray. Could have been dark blue."

He looked disappointed in her, and not for the first time. "You think whoever it was followed you from the hospital?"

She nodded. "I saw that blonde woman again at the hospital, coming out of Cody's room." She described her. Jaden made no comment as he pulled out his notebook and wrote it down. "I didn't see what she was driving, but it could have been her who tried to force me off the road."

Having him here made her feel better, stronger. She felt a little foolish for being so frightened earlier. So what if someone had followed her? They hadn't crashed into her. Maybe they were just trying to scare her. If it had been the blonde, she could have only been warning her to stay away from Cody.

Olivia knew it wasn't just today's incident that had her shaken. It was everything since she'd come home. She and Cody at the bar like old times, the disastrous trip to Starling that had ended so tragically, Jaden being the lead deputy on the case and the distance she felt between them.

Nothing had gone as she had wanted it to. That feeling of being a part of this town, her old friends, all of it was gone. She'd thought she could just fall back into that comfortable place she'd left behind. She couldn't have been more wrong.

What she should have done was go to see Jaden right away. She'd thought she had time to settle back in and sort out her feelings before she had to face him.

"You didn't recognize the SUV?" he asked and looked up from his notebook when she was so lost in her thoughts that she didn't answer right away. He repeated his question, studying her openly.

She shook her head. "You think it had something to do with the other night in Starling?" she asked Jaden.

He pocketed the notebook and pen. "I think you should be careful. Maybe stick closer to home."

She wanted to ask if he was close to finding Rob's killer and the person who'd attacked Cody, but hesitated. She didn't think he was or he wouldn't still be looking at her with suspicion. "Any news on Dean?"

"No. Dogs were brought in for the search because of all the tornado debris. His body wasn't found in Starling. It's possible, if he wasn't sheltered, that the tornado swept him away. They have widened their search."

Olivia could tell that Jaden had little hope of finding Dean alive. Her heart hurt to think about all of it. The tornado had been so destructive, but it hadn't caused Rob's death or Cody's concussion. Instead, the chances were that the killer was someone she knew. One of the old gang? That didn't leave many options. Emery? Or Dean?

She thought about the dark figure she'd glimpsed when she'd looked back at the Rusk house. It had appeared and disappeared so quickly, she'd thought she'd been seeing things. But what if she hadn't?

What if Elden Rusk had been there Halloween night?

JADEN HAD BEEN ANXIOUS to get back to town and was glad when Olivia's mother drove into the yard from her hair appointment. He was finding it harder and harder to be around his former fiancée. Only minutes ago, he'd had her in his arms. The memory made him ache. How could he forget the familiar feel of her body against his? He couldn't, and that was part of the problem.

When he'd thought he would never see her again, he'd thought that eventually he'd get over her. Now he knew he'd only been kidding himself.

"Remember what I said about being careful," he'd told her before driving away, unable to mask the edge to his voice. Why had she returned? Why had she gone to Starling? And the big question: Why had she gone with Cody?

He doubted she would listen to his advice as he left and drove into town, hoping to catch Krystal Lee at home. He'd recognized Krystal from Olivia's description she'd given of the blonde she'd seen at the hospital. The woman had not been home earlier, but he had a feeling she might be back by now.

Krystal Lee answered the door, wearing a robe. Her blond hair was wet and her feet bare. She was an attractive woman, except for her blue eyes. There was a brittle hardness there, as if she hadn't gotten what she'd wanted out of life and resented the devil out of it.

"Did I catch you at a bad time?" the deputy asked.

She smiled and leaned suggestively against the door frame. "Depends on what you have in mind."

"I need to ask you some questions. Perhaps you could get dressed. I don't mind waiting."

She pushed herself off the door frame, her smile vanishing. "Fine. I guess you'd better come in. You can wait out here in the living room." With that, she turned and disappeared down a hallway.

Jaden pushed the door all the way open and entered the house. He knew that she rented the small house, worked part-time at the convenience store and drove a small, compact, older-model car. She'd had four speeding tickets, but other than that, she'd kept her nose clean.

As he waited, he looked around since he assumed she was going to take her time. He spotted a pair of dirty boots by the door. Several jackets and coats hung above them, one jacket with fresh dirt on the sleeve. The house smelled like leftover pizza and the lingering scent of stale beer.

He was standing at the front window when she returned.

"I hope I didn't keep you waiting," she said snidely.

"Not at all." He turned to look at her and smiled. "I looked around while I was waiting." His gaze went to the dirty boots by the door as he pulled out his notebook and pen. "Let's start with where you were this morning." He turned in time to see her expression. It was enough to tell him she'd been up to no good.

Without her offering, he took a seat on the end of the couch and waited for her to sit. She had several options, one of two worn recliners or the other end of the equally worn couch. She chose the couch and turned toward him.

She'd changed into a T-shirt and jeans. Her feet were still bare, her hair pulled up in a ponytail. The look on her recently made-up face said he would have to drag the truth out of her.

"Why don't you start with what you were doing at the hospital this morning?" he said and clicked on his pen.

"Who said I was at the hospital?" she asked.

He waited, holding her gaze until she finally cursed and said, "That skinny nurse, huh."

"You were visiting Cody, and not for the first time," he said. "What's your relationship?"

"Relationship?" She made it sound as if she'd never heard the word before.

Again, he could have outwaited her, but was quickly losing his patience. "Maybe I should take you down to the sheriff's office for further questioning." He started to put his notebook and pen away, but she stopped him.

"Fine. Cody's my boyfriend. I have every right to see him."

"Does he know he's your boyfriend, because I believe he was with Olivia Brooks Halloween night?"

Her eyes narrowed into a glare, her jaw tightening before she said, *"He* knows, but apparently Olivia doesn't."

"Is that why you followed her when she left the hospital and tried to run her off the road?"

"I don't know what you're talking about," she snapped, leaning away from him and the accusation.

"I can have the dirt on your boots compared to that of the barrow pit where your SUV ended up," he said. "This time of year, it isn't quite mud, but close."

She grabbed on to the one thing she thought could save her and gave him a haughty look. "I don't own an SUV."

"No, but I'm betting you borrowed one." Before she could argue further, he asked, "Where were you Halloween night?"

The question caught her by surprise. Her eyes widened for a moment. "Home."

"Anyone with you?" She shook her head. "See any trick-or-treaters who can verify your story?"

"I had my lights turned off, so I didn't get any. Migraine headache. I went to bed early."

"You often get migraines?" Before she could answer, he said, "I can check with your doctor."

"My first migraine. Really a bitch."

"So I've heard." Seeing that he wasn't going to get any more from her, he put away his notebook and pen and stood. "I hope I don't have to come back and arrest you for anything, but I will be keeping an eye on you," he said as he walked to the door.

"Thanks. I appreciate that," she said sarcastically as he left.

Jaden didn't have to go far. A few blocks away, he stopped at the home of Jenny and Tom Lee. Tom's truck wasn't parked in the drive and neither was Jenny's car. But when he got out and looked in the garage, he found a dark gray SUV. He'd been bluffing back at Krystal's about comparing the dirt on her boots with that of the dirt in the barrow pit near Olivia's mother's house.

But even peering through the dusty garage door windows, he could see the large SUV's tires were caked with fresh earth.

OLIVIA HADN'T BEEN anxious to go back into the house after the deputy left and her mother went inside. She'd lived in this community for seventeen years before she'd left for college and hadn't returned until a few days ago. She'd never been afraid. But then, she'd never had anyone who'd wanted to run her off the road.

Her cell rang. She saw it was Jaden and felt her pulse jump like it used to when he called, back when they were together. She had loved the sound of his voice, been lulled by it. She let it ring again before she picked up, reminding herself that he was probably calling because he was a deputy and she was a suspect.

"Hello?"

"Hey," he said in a familiar way that set her pulse off again. "I just wanted to let you know that you shouldn't be having any more trouble from the person who threatened you earlier."

"You know who it was?" She heard him hesitate.

"It had nothing to do with Starling and what happened up there. Just a jealous girlfriend of Cody's."

"The blonde from the hospital. Who is she?"

"Krystal Lee. She's Tom Lee's sister, Jenny's sister-in-law. But I've spoken to her. I think that's the last you have to worry about her," he said.

Olivia wondered about that, given how aggressive she'd been on the road earlier. "You didn't arrest her?"

"No, not enough evidence to do that. I warned her. Just didn't want you to worry."

Good luck with that, she thought. "Any news about what happened at Starling?" She realized she was trying to keep him on the phone. Just the sound of his voice made her feel better. She'd missed it.

"Not yet. I'm getting another call. If you… Gotta go." And he was gone.

She stood holding the phone. If you…what? What had he stopped himself from saying?

"You going to stand outside all day?" her mother called from the porch.

Olivia pocketed her phone, turned and headed for the house. She could feel her mother's questioning gaze on her.

"Who was that on the phone?" her mother asked.

"Jaden. It wasn't anything." She stepped into the house, knowing her mother wasn't going to let it go. She headed for the kitchen to make herself a sandwich, her mother on her heels. "You want a sandwich?"

"I ate in town. What did Jaden want?"

Digging out what she needed from the refrigerator, she said, "Earlier, someone followed me from the hospital, running up behind me like she was going to run me off the road."

"She?"

"Cody's girlfriend, Krystal Lee."

Her mother's expression told volumes as to how she felt about Krystal Lee. "Cody forgot to mention he had a girlfriend when he asked you out for Halloween night?" Sharon shook her head. "You still worried she'll come after you again?"

Olivia concentrated on slicing a tomato before she answered. "I'm not worried." That wasn't entirely true, but she didn't want her mother doing something foolish like going over to Krystal's house and threatening her. It wouldn't be the first time her mother had done something like that.

"So why do you look worried?"

She spread mayo on the bread, then layered on ham, cheese, lettuce and sliced tomato. "It's the whole Starling thing," she said as she completed her task and reached for one of the small bags of chips her mother kept on hand. "What if he never finds out who killed Rob and injured Cody?" she added as she sat down at the kitchen table. She took a bite of her sandwich.

"Jaden doesn't really think you had anything to do with that," her mother said as she joined her at the table. "He's just angry at you for breaking off the engagement."

Olivia looked up, finished chewing and set down her sandwich. "I didn't break it off. Jaden did."

"What?"

She shook her head. "He didn't think I was ready to get married—let alone to him." She'd seldom seen her mother unable to speak.

"Why would he think that?" Sharon Brooks finally asked.

"I don't know what he thinks. He was headed to law school. I'd just gotten my job I'd hoped for. We were going in separate directions. I suggested postponing the wedding."

"Law school? How'd he end up being a deputy in Fortune Creek?"

"Turns out we both changed our minds about what we wanted to do," Olivia said.

"Was he right about you not being ready?" Before Olivia could answer, her mother said, "Well, obviously, because the first thing you did when you got back here was to go out with Cody Ryan, your high school boyfriend."

"It wasn't like that," she protested, knowing how it looked. She regretted it more than she could say. "We're just friends."

Her mother had always preferred anyone over Cody, saying she couldn't bear seeing her daughter organizing nuts and bolts down at the hardware store for the rest of her life. *What kind of life can he offer you? You think Cody and his dad wouldn't have you working down there in the hardware store?*

"I guess it wouldn't make that much difference, working at a hardware store or being the wife of a deputy and living all the way up there in Fortune Creek," her mother said now.

Olivia groaned. "Well, that's not going to happen."

"But for some reason both men thought you were going to marry them," her mother just had to point out. "One of them must be the reason you're back home."

Pushing her sandwich away, she snapped, "Do we have to talk about my past mistakes?"

"Only if you keep making the same ones," her mother quipped.

"I just wanted to hang out with some old friends Halloween night. Cody and I used to be friends. He was my best friend for a lot of years. I thought we could have that again. I was wrong."

"I should say so since now one of your old friends is dead, Cody's in the hospital and another friend is missing."

She shook her head, telling herself that her mother had good intentions and was only trying to protect her. "I just came from the hospital. Cody has regained consciousness, but he doesn't remember anything. He didn't even remember I was back in town."

Her mother got up from the table, returning with a knife. Olivia watched her cut the sandwich in two before sitting down to eat it. "I didn't have much for lunch," she said, grinning before taking a bite.

Olivia opened the bag of chips, dumping them on the side of the plate so her mother could reach them. She picked up the other half with her one bite out of it. Sometimes she wished she couldn't remember the past.

"I love them both," she said between bites. "Cody just as a friend. Jaden…" Her voice broke with emotion. "I can't seem to get over him. All right? It's why I came home."

Her mother nodded, smiled and reached over with her free hand to squeeze her daughter's. "That's what I thought. Don't worry. You'll figure it out."

Her laugh sounded more scared than bitter. "If only it were that easy."

"What a problem. If it's Jaden you're in love with, then I guess you'd better let him know you're serious. If you are…"

Olivia nodded. "But right now, he just sees me as a suspect in a murder investigation." She didn't mention that him finding her on a night out with Cody hadn't helped, and neither did her mother. She'd been such a fool to think she could recapture the fun times she and Cody had in high school for even one night.

Her phone pinged. It was a text from Emery. He wanted to meet her at the bar. Said it was important.

Chapter Ten

Emery was the last person Olivia had expected to hear from. They'd been friends but never close growing up. She'd hesitated before responding, wondering what he could want. Jaden had told her to stay close to home, and after the road race with Krystal Lee, she was inclined to do just that.

The problem was that, earlier, at the hospital, Jaden had asked for her help. *Someone's lying*, he'd said.

She was curious why Emery wanted to meet. What was so important?

"I'm going to meet a friend," she told her mother as she quickly left to avoid her questioning whether going into town tonight after what had happened was a bad idea. Olivia was already questioning it herself as she drove to the bar.

It was one of those pitch-black nights when the clouds hung low, blotting out the stars. She could barely see the outline of the mountains that rimmed the valley against the dark sky. Like her future, all she could see was the few feet her headlights illuminated ahead of her. When she finally caught the lights of town, she relaxed a little and tried not to think about the ride home.

There were only a few cars in the bar parking lot because of the time of the year and the weekday night. She found Emery sitting in a corner booth at the back, alone. He was staring into his half-empty glass and didn't look up until she slid into the booth, across from him.

He seemed startled to see her for a moment. She'd never seen him nervous, let alone on edge. Until tonight.

"Has something happened?" she whispered.

"Let me get you a drink," he said, hurriedly getting to his feet. "What would you like?"

Thinking of her drive home, she said, "Just a cola."

He hurried away to the bar and came back a few minutes later with her soda and another drink for himself. He took a gulp of his before he said, "You heard about the human bones that were found?"

"Cody and I discovered them after the tornado left them exposed down in the root cellar."

"They're Evangeline's. I have a friend who works at the sheriff's office."

"I'm surprised they already have the DNA back," she said.

Emery shook his head. "They don't, but there was some clothing found buried deeper in the grave that matched what Evangeline was wearing the night she disappeared."

Olivia shuddered, thinking of the dark figure she'd seen standing in the Rusk doorway. "It's so creepy. Do they think she's been there this whole time?"

Emery nodded and took another slug of his drink. "There was a man buried with her. Probably the father of her baby." He raised an eyebrow. "You know he killed his daughter and the man who'd impregnated her."

She didn't know that for a fact, although it did seem likely, didn't it? Was this why Emery had gotten her here tonight? He could have told her in the text.

"There's something I didn't tell anyone about that night,"

Emery said as he ran his finger through the moisture on his glass without looking at her. "I saw him."

"Saw who?" She realized she was whispering, although there was no one around who could hear. The only patrons were a handful at the bar. The bartender had the television on a loud ball game.

Emery looked up at her. "Elden Rusk."

She didn't know what to say, but she could understand why he hadn't mentioned this to anyone, maybe especially Jaden. She certainly hadn't told anyone what she thought she'd seen. "When was that?"

"When I was looking for Rob. The wind was so strong, it had knocked me down. I looked up and there he was, all dressed in black, his head covered by a big hat."

She swallowed the lump in her throat. "You're sure it was him?"

He nodded, not at all upset that she would question him. "It wasn't the first time I've seen him. I'd know those eyes anywhere."

"You'd seen him before?"

Emery took another gulp of his drink. His hand shook as he replaced the glass. He seemed to be avoiding her eyes. "When I was a kid, I used to ride my bike out to Starling. The houses were all empty, everyone gone, but, like you said, creepy. It always bothered us that the people left so quickly, leaving a lot of their stuff behind."

"Us?" she asked.

"Rob and me. We used to joke that a spaceship zapped them all up." He toyed with his glass that was now almost empty. "We used to talk all the time about what we would do when we found Rusk's gold." He looked up then, his gaze connecting with hers. "We saw him. He was loading something into the back of his old truck. We sneaked up on him, but he saw us."

Emery turned then toward the bar. "Could use another drink over here," he called before he finished what was in his glass and looked at her again.

Olivia realized she'd been holding her breath.

"Rusk picked up an old rusty shovel and came after us. Rob could always run faster than me. I'd never run so fast in my life, but it wasn't fast enough. Rusk caught me, dragging me to the ground. He lifted that old shovel. I thought he was going to kill me. If Rob hadn't come back when he had…"

The bartender dropped off his drink and took his empties. "How about you?" he said to Olivia, who could only shake her head. She hadn't even touched her cola.

"Rob saved you?" she said when Emery didn't continue.

"He grabbed the shovel and brought it down on the man's head. Knocked him out cold. My legs were so weak, I could barely stand. I was shaking all over. I thought Rob had killed him, but we went back the next day. Elden and his old truck were gone. But I'll never forget the look on that man's face when he raised that shovel. He was going to kill me and would have if not for Rob." Emery picked up his drink and took a healthy gulp.

"Why are you telling me this?"

"Because," he said as he put down his glass, "Rob saved my life. I would never have hurt him, let alone killed him. But I know who did. It had to be Rusk. I thought I saw him right as the tornado hit. I swear it was him, all dressed in black, his head covered. He looked right at me."

"Why didn't you tell the deputy this?" she asked.

He scoffed. "Come on. Who would believe me? How many times have people said they saw Elden Rusk out at Starling? I'd be the laughingstock, but worse, the deputy would think I was trying to save my own skin. Other than whoever killed him, I was one of the last people to see Rob alive."

Olivia took a sip of her cola before she had to ask again, "Why are you telling *me*?"

"I don't know. I needed to tell someone who might believe me. Didn't I hear that you once saw Rusk out at Starling?"

She suspected his motivation had more to do with having heard she'd been engaged to Deputy Sheriff Jaden Montgomery. "You think Rusk recognized Rob as the kid who'd coldcocked him and that's why he killed him?"

"Why not? If you had seen the look in that man's eyes when he had me down on the ground with that shovel in his hands…"

"You said he was loading something into his truck."

Emery nodded. "Something heavy like…gold bars."

"Then why would you and Rob still be looking for gold at Starling if Rusk had taken it?"

"Because we think he hid it all over the side of the mountain," Emery said. "Maybe he didn't get it all."

"Are you really telling me that, after Rob knocked Rusk out, you didn't go see what he'd loaded in the back of his truck?"

"We were terrified we'd killed him."

"Even more reason to take the time to see what he had loaded in the truck."

Emery looked away, seeming defeated. "It wasn't gold. It was a bunch of old scrap iron he'd scavenged from the place."

She let out a huff. "Did you and Rob start the rumor about the gold?" she demanded, pretty sure they had.

"I think I heard it before that," he hedged. "The thing is, I didn't kill Rob. I had no reason to."

"You should tell the deputy. Coming from me wouldn't carry any weight. I'm a suspect as well as you."

Emery drained his drink and sighed. "Well, it was good to get it off my chest. I appreciate you listening."

"Thanks for the cola." She took another drink of it to be polite as she wondered if that was all Emery had wanted to tell her. She couldn't help feeling like there was a lot more. "So, you and Rob have been good friends all these years." He nodded, seeming a little distracted. "I know the deputy asked, but did Dean get along with Rob?"

"He and Dean were tight. It wasn't one of us." He lowered his voice. "It was Rusk."

She felt a chill and was about to ask Emery if he could follow her home when he got a call. He excused himself and stepped away from the booth, leaving her to mull over what he'd told her. That he was running scared didn't surprise her. His best friend had been murdered, and like her, he was a suspect.

"I'm sorry. I have to go," he said when he returned. He looked even more nervous than he had earlier.

"Is everything all right?" she asked. Clearly, it wasn't.

"Fine. It's a friend who needs my help. Thanks so much for coming in and listening. You believed me, didn't you?" She nodded and he smiled. "I hope things work out with you and Cody." He grabbed up his jacket and headed for the door before she could tell him things weren't going to work out between her and Cody—at least, not the way Emery probably hoped.

The bar was even more empty than it had been, the night even darker as she stepped outside. She couldn't help feeling spooked after everything that had happened. She hurried across the nearly-empty parking lot, anxious to reach her car.

She was already opening the door and about to climb in when she realized she wasn't going anywhere. In the glow of the neon bar sign, she saw that her driver's-side front tire was flat. There was a screwdriver sticking out of the side of it.

IT WAS LATE when Jaden got the call. He hadn't expected to hear from Olivia again so soon and was immediately worried. "What's wrong?"

"I need your help," she said, her fear making his skyrocket. "I'm in the bar parking lot. My tire is flat. Someone stuck a screwdriver in it."

Bar parking lot? Hadn't he advised her to stay close to home? He didn't have to ask which bar. "I'll be right there."

The motel where he was staying while in town on the case wasn't far from the bar where Olivia had said she'd met up with Cody and her old friends the night they decided to spend Halloween at Starling.

He found her sitting in her car in the almost-empty lot and pulled alongside in his patrol SUV, spotting the flat tire. She climbed out into the night at once. He couldn't tell if she was more scared or angry.

"What are you doing here?" he demanded when what he really wanted to know was who she'd been with at the bar. Cody Ryan had been released from the hospital. Had he felt up to going to the bar his first night home?

"What you asked me to do," she snapped, clearly not liking the tone of his voice.

"I believe I asked you to stay close to home."

"Before that, you asked me to keep my ear to the ground

with my old friends," she said. "Emery texted me. He said it was important."

Jaden pulled off his hat and raked a hand through his hair. Not Cody. He hated that he was jealous. He had no right to be, but that didn't stop him.

"Sorry. Why don't you go back into the bar? I'll join you when I'm finished here." He pulled on a latex glove before opening an evidence bag. She watched him remove the screwdriver from the tire and drop it in the bag.

"I'd rather stay out here," she said as he secured the bag in his SUV, then opened her car door and pulled the lever that opened her trunk. "Emery says he didn't kill Rob because he owed him his life."

As he changed her tire, he listened to the story she said Emery had related to her in the bar. When she finished, he asked, "Why didn't he come to me with this? Why you?"

"I asked him that. He didn't think you would believe him."

Jaden couldn't argue with that. Being suspicious came with the job, but he found himself more interested in where Emery had taken off to from the bar. "Doesn't it seem suspicious that he gets you into town, takes off suddenly, and you find your tire punctured in the lot? He didn't tell you why he had to leave so quickly?"

She shrugged, arms crossed over her chest, and looked upset that he wasn't more interested in Emery's story about seeing Rusk on Halloween night at Starling. "He said a friend needed him. Why would he flatten my tire?" Good question, he thought. "You don't believe him, do you?"

"I didn't say that." He replaced her jack and loaded the ruined tire in the back before slamming the lid. "You'll want to get a new tire tomorrow."

"Thanks for your help." She started toward her car,

clearly intending to get in and drive home. But she'd have to get him to move out of the way to do so.

"You have no idea who called Emery?" he asked.

"No." She frowned. "Maybe. It sounded like he was talking to a woman."

Jaden nodded. "One of those girls from Halloween?"

She shook her head. "Older, more like someone he knew well. But I'm just going by his tone of voice. That's all I could make out."

OLIVIA REALIZED THAT Jaden seemed in no hurry to leave. What was he waiting for? "You know I wouldn't have called unless—"

"You needed me. You can always call. I hope you know that."

The cloudy darkness felt almost intimate as they stood looking at each other. The music coming from the bar seemed louder than it had been. The neon bar sign threw shadows across the parking lot. She stood only inches from him, feeling the intensity of his gaze.

"You're in my way," she said, her words coming out in a whisper.

"Remember this song?" he asked, cocking his head to listen to the music coming from the bar.

As if Olivia could have forgotten the song, let alone forget being in his arms slow dancing. It had been something they'd done often when they were dating. A song would come on, and no matter where they were, he would reach for her.

Like now. He reached for her in the darkness as she said, "We used to dance to this."

Without a thought, she slipped into his arms. He drew her close, the two of them moving to the rhythm as they danced between the two vehicles as if they'd been doing it for years. She could feel his breath in her hair. She closed her eyes, relishing his hard body, the strength of his arms around her. This was the one place she'd ever felt truly safe and secure.

In his arms, she'd had no doubts. She'd known what she'd wanted and needed—something she apparently couldn't have since he'd broken off their engagement.

The song ended and she pulled back to look up at him in the dim glow of the bar sign. The urge to kiss him was so strong that she felt herself leaning in, her lips only a breath away when a horn blared, making them both jump apart. Headlights washed over them as a pickup pulled into the parking lot.

Jaden swore under his breath. "We need to get you home. I'll follow you."

It was exactly what she wanted, yet she started to tell him it wasn't necessary. One look at his expression and she knew it would be a fight she'd lose. It was a relief. She nodded since she'd been dreading the drive home.

Jaden opened her car door. His hand brushed her shoulder as she climbed in, sending shivers up her arms. They'd been so close to kissing. Why did she believe in her heart that with one kiss, he would know that they belonged together?

Foolishness, she told herself as she started the engine and pulled out, Jaden right behind her. The glow of his headlights behind her seemed to warm the dark autumn night even more as she drove toward home.

Her body still quaked, emotions running hot and wild. Being in his arms... Holding her like that, dancing, he had to remember how good they were together. She couldn't get the almost-kiss out of her mind or the ache of disappointment that they'd been interrupted. She wondered if Jaden was feeling the same way right now and shook her head.

You need to tell him how you feel.

"Now? I'm a suspect in his murder investigation. Do you really think right now is the time?" she demanded of herself.

No answer, which was an answer in itself, wasn't it?

"You really need to quit talking to yourself, too," she said and glanced in the rearview mirror to see his headlights. They stayed a safe distance behind her until she turned into her mother's driveway and parked.

Jaden pulled in behind her. For a moment, she thought he might get out, but instead, he flashed his lights and then left.

She felt bereft as she watched his vehicle lights disappear down the road. "Don't let one dance make you think anything has changed," she said to herself. She was still a suspect and would be until the killer was caught.

But she knew it wasn't just that keeping her and Jaden apart. She'd known this wouldn't be easy. Wasn't that why she hadn't gone straight to Jaden when she'd returned home? She hadn't been able to stand the thought that he might turn her away and not hear her out.

Patience, she told herself with a sigh. But even as she thought it, her only other option had to be something besides hanging out here at the house with her mother watching her every minute, wondering what she was doing with her life. She needed to figure out who'd killed Rob, who'd attacked Cody, who'd flattened her tire. And maybe why Emery had left the bar so fast when he'd gotten that call.

As her mother came out on the porch, she cut her engine and lights, and climbed out, determined to clear herself.

JADEN CURSED HIMSELF all the way back to town. What was he doing? Just racing headlong toward heartbreak. He'd broken off the engagement because he'd felt in his heart that Livie wasn't ready. Did he really believe that something had changed? She'd come back to town and gone straight to her old boyfriend. Her going out with Cody the minute she'd hit town… What more proof did he need?

But dancing with her, holding her in his arms, almost kissing, had felt so right. He'd wanted that kiss desperately. Like one kiss was going to chase away any doubts he still had.

Yet just before they'd almost kissed, he'd looked into her eyes and he'd known heart deep that she still loved him. He couldn't be wrong about that. Not that it meant she'd ever want to be the wife of a small-town deputy.

He slammed his hand into the steering wheel. He didn't have time for this. He had a job to do. Determined to concentrate on work, he recalled what Livie had told him about Emery. He didn't know what to believe. Emery's story sounded like boys would be boys. Did he believe Elden Rusk had planned to kill Emery and Rob with a shovel? He thought of the boogeyman from his nightmares while living in Starling. Maybe.

Rusk had scared him as a boy. It was the man's eyes. When they lit on you, it felt as if he could smite you on the spot. Jaden had been terrified of him. He couldn't imagine what he would have done if Rusk had ever brandished a rusted shovel at him.

Yet something felt off about Emery summoning Olivia to the bar to tell her about his and Rob's run-in with Rusk—especially with someone flattening her tire. Could it have been some kids looking for trouble? Unfortunately, he didn't believe it. Krystal? Maybe. He cursed at the thought since he'd told Livie that he had handled it.

The woman kept crowding his thoughts, reminding him of her in his arms, in his bed, always in his head and still lodged deep in his heart. He needed to stay away from her, but he was working a murder investigation—and Livie was right there, right in the center.

He should never have taken her in his arms to dance. He should definitely have not almost kissed her. Especially in public and not in the middle of an investigation involving her. He didn't know who had been in that pickup that had pulled into the bar parking lot, but he knew how quickly word spread in this town. The deputy and his suspect just a breath away from kissing in the parking lot would be all over town by morning.

The worst part was that he had wanted that damn kiss more than his next breath and now he couldn't get it out of his head. He kept remembering their deep, long kisses, the passion they'd ignited, their need for each other. Olivia Brooks had done more than stolen his heart. She'd ruined him for any other woman.

So why in the hell hadn't he ignored his doubts and married her? If he'd offered to follow her to her job— He pushed the thought away. She hadn't wanted that, or she would have suggested it. She'd needed her freedom to chase her dream. She'd needed it more than him. But what about now?

He knew he wasn't going to be able to sleep. It didn't help when he got a call the moment he walked into his rental.

Elden Rusk had been found.

Chapter Eleven

Olivia hadn't been inside the hardware store in years. It had the same smell, the same narrow aisles between high shelves loaded with every household necessity she could name and many she couldn't.

She wasn't surprised to find Cody working. Apparently, he had the same schedule he'd had in high school. Just like he'd never missed a day of school or work, he hadn't let a concussion keep him from his spot behind the counter.

The bandage on his head had been replaced with a smaller one. Like her, he still had the scrapes and scratches, the bruises and bumps on his face and arms. But unlike her, he looked pale.

"What are you doing working?" she demanded, unable to stop herself. She glanced around for his father and didn't see him.

"Dad had to run an errand. I'm just filling in until he gets back," Cody said. His voice softened as he asked, "How are you doing?"

"Fine." She reminded herself that the reason she was there was that he'd lied to her. "You didn't tell me you had a girlfriend."

He reddened. "Krystal isn't… We aren't… That is, we—"

"She tried to run me off the road yesterday."

"No. Seriously?" He shook his head. "I'm sorry. She's a little hot-tempered and unpredictable sometimes, but she's not dangerous."

"Are you sure about that?" she said, noticing a basketful of screwdrivers on sale. "After that, someone flattened my tire with one of your sale items here."

He swore. "I'll talk to her."

"The deputy already did. He didn't think she'd give me any more trouble. Apparently, he was wrong." She met his stare and felt her anger dissolve. This man had once been her best friend. She still cared about Cody. "Has your memory come back?"

"Bits and pieces. Nothing I can understand."

"It does make me wonder what Krystal would have done if she'd caught you out in Starling with me."

His hand went to his head and the dressing over the wound. "She wouldn't..." His words dropped off as his father came in through the back to relieve him.

"I should get going. But one question before I go... Did Krystal have something against Rob or Dean?"

Cody made an impatient face. "I'm sorry the two of you got into it, but Krystal isn't like that."

"Keep telling yourself that," she said and left.

ELDEN RUSK WAS alive and staying in an assisted-living facility in Kalispell. Not that far from Starling, the deputy noted. It was a pleasant enough drive this morning, the sun sparkling on the dew in the thick pines that bordered each side of the road. The mountains shone against a cloudless blue sky. The air smelled of fall, just cool enough to remind him that winter wasn't far behind. He didn't want to even think about a long, cold winter in Fortune Creek after seeing Livie again.

He found the facility without any trouble. It was one level, brick, and on the edge of town. There were benches still outside under the pines. But they were all empty this morning.

Jaden pushed through the front door and into the lobby, heading for the reception desk. "Hello. I'm looking for Elden Rusk," he said to the young dark-haired woman sitting there.

"Room 214," she said without looking up from her paperwork.

"Thank you."

He started to turn and head down the hallway in front of him when she called, "Other way." He swiveled, passing a woman leaning on her walker. In a large room, he saw a few elderly people playing cards at a table. A television was on in the room. Several women were sitting in front of it but didn't seem to be watching the game show that was playing.

He found Elden's room at the end of another hallway. The door was closed. He knocked. Hearing no response, he knocked again, then looked down the empty hall before he tried the door.

Earlier, he'd seen a couple of women in scrubs he took for staff, but no one paid him any mind or asked where he was going. The knob turned in his hand. He pushed and the door swung open.

At first, all he saw was blinding brightness from the sun streaming through the large window. He'd expected to see the Elden Rusk he remembered from when he and his parents had lived in Starling. A large, gruff man with a tuft of dirty-blond hair and piercing blue eyes. The boogeyman.

But the man sitting in front of the window was shrunken and bald. Or maybe it was the wheelchair he was slumped in that made him look so small and harmless. The only thing that was the same were those ice-blue eyes when Rusk turned to look at him standing in the doorway.

in that room that could be used, that might tie Elden Rusk to what he'd seen the night they'd had confrontation or when a ran-back to his truck and driven to the sheriff.

Chapter Twelve

As Jaden drove toward the hospital, the sun rose high over the snowcapped mountain peaks, casting a glow over the Montana landscape. He hardly noticed. His mind had been on little else but this case since it had begun. The case and Olivia.

He couldn't quit thinking about the story Emery had told Olivia. He kept asking himself why Emery hadn't come to him with it. Why tell Olivia? Something felt off and had since the beginning.

He'd been as ready as Emery to blame Rusk for what had happened out there Halloween night. But after seeing the man again, he knew that whoever Emery might have seen, it hadn't been Elden Rusk.

Jaden had attempted to tell the man about what had been unearthed. Along with the clothing found with the bones, he let him know that there was no doubt that they belonged to Evangeline.

"He can't understand you," the nurse had said when she'd found Jaden in Rusk's room. "Advanced dementia."

"I thought that, when he first saw me, he might have recognized me."

She shook her head. "I'm sorry. Are you a relative?"

"No, we haven't seen each other for years. I had some

news for him." But when he'd tried to tell Rusk about Evangeline, the man had looked blankly at him. When Jaden had tried again, Rusk had become agitated, tried to say something, spittle on his lips as he'd begun to moan loudly.

The nurse suggested Jaden take a walk around the facility and try again. "You might have better luck later."

He questioned whether or not Rusk had understood about his daughter's remains being found. But one thing was clear. Elden Rusk hadn't been out at Starling on Halloween night. If Emery was telling the truth, though, someone had wanted him to believe Rusk was alive and out for blood. It would have been easy enough to dress in all black, head covered with a big, floppy black hat, and try to frighten the group partying in the abandoned community. Given the storm and the confusion, it would have made revenge easier. Someone had taken advantage. Someone was lying.

Maybe they were all lying.

OLIVIA WAS SURPRISED to get a text from Cody later that afternoon. Her mother was watching one of her favorite old black-and-white movies in the other room.

I need to talk to you. It's important. Meet me?

She glanced into the living room. Her mother was laughing and motioning for Olivia to join her. "You really should watch this."

"I've seen it. Not as many times as you have, but enough," she said as she walked into the room. "I might run into town and get some things from the grocery store."

"We have ice cream. What else do we need?"

She smiled at her mother. She loved seeing her this content. Was it from giving up on men, on love? Olivia suspected it just might be. She hesitated, not sure that meeting Cody was a good idea. Worse, not telling her mother the truth about where she was going might also be a mistake.

But she wasn't up to an argument, especially when her mother was in such a good mood. "I won't be long," she said and headed for the door.

"We could always use more ice cream," her mother called. "Chocolate!"

The door closed behind her. As she walked to her car, Olivia still hesitated to text him back. She felt as if she and Cody had said everything they'd needed to.

When he texted back to meet him at the park down by the river after he got off work, she was glad she'd hesitated. Apparently, he was back at the hardware store. She couldn't imagine why he wanted to see her after what they'd said to each other Halloween night—let alone at the hardware store before.

Then she recalled that he had little to no memory of Halloween.

She figured she could kill some time in town before she met him.

JADEN HAD TAKEN the nurse's advice. He'd walked around, circling back to Elden Rusk's room after he'd had his lunch.

Elden looked up the moment the deputy walked into the room. This time, Jaden was sure the old man recognized him. He pulled up a chair in front of the wheelchair.

"I'm Deputy Jaden Montgomery," he said. "We believe your daughter Evangeline's remains have been found in a root cellar in Starling." He was unsure of what kind of response he would get—if any.

"Too pretty," the man rasped. "Tried to warn her mother. Evangeline—" His voice broke. "My sweet Evangeline."

Eyes narrowing, he said, his voice gruff, "Tried to protect her. They came like bees to honey." His eyes filled with tears.

Jaden had to ask. "Did you kill her?"

Rusk seemed to freeze, his gaze foggy with tears and memories. "Too pretty. Tried to warn her mother." He coughed and fell silent. Jaden thought that was all the man was going to say.

He rose to leave when Rusk said, "Criminal— Did what had to be done... Destroyed everything." He began to cry in chest-heaving gulps, the noise bringing a different nurse into the room.

"I gave him some sad news," the deputy said. "About his daughter. It's part of a murder investigation."

"Evangeline," the nurse said as she put an arm around the man to try to soothe him. "I heard on the news that her body had been found. Broke my heart."

"Did he ever tell you what happened?" Jaden asked.

She hesitated a moment. "She was murdered?" He nodded. Sighing, she said, "When he was first brought here, he talked about her. He didn't say it in so many words, but it seems she'd gotten pregnant at sixteen but refused to tell him who the father of her unborn baby was. Apparently, some man in the community where they lived."

The other body in the root-cellar grave, Jaden thought.

"I think what's haunted him all these years was that he never knew who the man was. When she disappeared... Well, he seemed to think they'd run away together, and he never saw her again."

"You know he started a community called Starling up in northeastern Montana. When Evangeline disappeared at sixteen, he walked away from it and the community died," Jaden said. "He'd started Starling to escape the outside world. He'd built his utopia, only to have what happened to his daughter and some man in the community destroy his dream. Has he ever mentioned his wife?"

"No. I got the impression she's been out of his life for a long time. A neighbor was the one who brought him in here."

The deputy stared at the old man in the wheelchair.

He didn't look much like a murderer. Nor a boogeyman anymore. He looked like a broken man haunted by his past and what he'd done as he quit sobbing and stared out the window, his blue eyes glazed over.

Jaden stopped in a small café after he left Elden Rusk's assisted-living facility. Seeing Rusk like that had unsettled him. It was the man's eyes. No matter what the nurse had said, Jaden couldn't shake the feeling that Rusk had recognized him.

He was leaving the café when he got the call. Dean Marsh had been found wandering down a road, miles from Starling. He was being treated for his injuries at the Kalispell hospital.

"Keep him there," he said. "I'm in town. I'll be right over."

WHEN HE WALKED into the hospital room, he found Dean sitting up, wolfing down lunch with a fork clutched in his left hand. His right arm was in a cast. Like the other Starling tornado survivors, he had cuts and bruises. But unlike them, he'd been missing since Halloween night.

Jaden pulled up a chair next to the bed and dragged out his notebook and pen. "Glad to see you've turned up," he said as Dean finished his lunch and pushed the tray away.

"I haven't eaten in days," he said, his voice gravelly. He took a sip of water from the glass on the table next to his bed.

"Where have you been since Halloween?"

Dean stared at him for a moment, as if considering the question. "When was Halloween?"

"A few days ago."

"Really? I don't know. I remember waking up in a ditch. I didn't know where I was or how I'd gotten there. My arm was broken, I knew that. I found a piece of wood and ripped off part of my shirt to make a splint. Then I just started walking."

"What do you remember before waking up in the ditch?"

Dean frowned and reached up to touch the bandage on his head. "Not much."

Memory loss. There seemed to be a lot of that going around, Jaden considered, questioning Dean's story. He recalled what Dean's wife, Angie, had said about her husband reappearing soon with some fantastic story about where he'd been. "You remember Halloween night?"

His frown deepened. "Halloween."

"You'd gone to Starling with some friends."

"Starling?" He sounded surprised by that.

"There was a storm." There appeared to be no recognition in Dean's expression. "A tornado."

"No kidding?" He shook his head. "Sorry, I don't remember a storm. Is everyone else all right?"

Not everyone, he thought as a nurse came in to take Dean down for more tests and Jaden left.

WHILE THE SUN had set, it wouldn't be dark for a couple of hours yet. Olivia drove to the spot where Cody's dad used to drop them off on weekends. The Ryans had the property next door, so Cody's dad would pick Olivia up on his way to town to work at the hardware store. She and Cody used to spend hours by the river skipping rocks and wading in the water until he returned—or her mother got worried and would come to take her home.

Too cold for playing in the water now, she mused as she parked next to his SUV and climbed out. She felt a chill and wasn't sure if it was the time of year—or finding out what was so important that they had to meet here. Jaden thought she hadn't gotten over her high school boyfriend. Meeting him down here at the river would only reinforce that misconception, but there was nothing she could do about that.

How could she explain that Cody was part of her every memory of growing up here? He'd always been there for her. Look how he'd been during the tornado. He'd saved her life. How could she not care about him?

She spotted him sitting on top of a picnic table close to the river's edge, chucking rocks out into the water as she walked up. "You came," he said, sounding surprised. Or maybe it was just relieved. She recalled the argument they'd had that night in Starling. Even if he couldn't remember Halloween, she knew he was still upset with her for leaving him and this town.

When they'd seen each other at the hardware store earlier, she'd been angry with him. She hadn't wanted to leave it like that. "What's up?"

"You want to sit?" he asked as he moved over to give her room.

"I'm fine standing."

"You're still mad at me," he said, nodding to himself. "Not that I blame you. I should have told you about Krystal."

"I wouldn't have gone to Starling with you if you had."

He chuckled. "Probably why I didn't tell you. I wanted to spend some time with you."

She had wanted the same thing. "You weren't very happy with me Halloween night."

"Sorry, I don't remember," he said, giving her an embarrassed grin. "But I'm sure I said some things I shouldn't have. I was hurt when you left."

"I know, but you've moved on, and I'm sure Krystal wasn't the first."

He gave her a bashful look. "You know me so well."

"If this is what you wanted to talk to me about—"

"No," he said, hopping off the table to walk down to the water's edge. He picked up a rock and skipped it across the dark surface of the cold river before turning to look at her. "I'm hoping you can help me remember what happened."

"You really still don't remember any of it?"

He shook his head. "I've talked to Emery. I know we all went out to Starling, there was a tornado, you and I were trapped in a root cellar. Somehow, you got out and went for help, and when you came back, I was unconscious and bleeding. That about cover it?"

"Pretty much, except for the part where you saved my life. We would have been killed if you hadn't talked me into going down into that root cellar to begin with. When the tornado hit, you pulled some heavy shelves over us and sheltered me with your body."

"Wow, I can't believe I did all that."

She smiled. "Yes, you can. It sounds just like you. You like being a hero."

That made him laugh, but it was as if he were holding back.

"Are you worried that whoever attacked you will try again?" she asked.

"I hadn't thought of that… Thanks. Something more to worry about."

"I'm serious. I can tell something's bothering you."

He looked at the ground for a few moments before he said, "When you went for help, did you see anyone?"

"No."

"How about when you came back?" She shook her head. "You came back alone, didn't you? Ahead of the others?"

"Yes." She frowned. "How did you know that?"

He shrugged. "I thought I heard you calling my name in this dream I had when I was in the hospital. I figured it must have been when I was unconscious because, in the dream, I couldn't answer."

"Maybe your subconscious is trying to remember."

"Maybe. Are they finished searching out at Starling?" he asked. "I thought maybe Jaden might have mentioned."

"Why?" She couldn't help her surprise. "You wouldn't go back out there, would you?"

"If it would help me remember, of course I would. You have no idea what it's like not knowing what happened, who attacked me and why."

"Maybe once Jaden finds out who killed Rob, that will help fill in some of the blanks for all of us."

"Yeah, it might have been the same person who attacked me."

"You have no idea why someone would want to hurt either of you?"

He met her gaze. "Not a clue. That's why I have to remember."

She thought about Jaden saying "Someone's lying" and felt as if the temperature had suddenly dropped. How could she have forgotten that whoever had attacked Cody was probably still a threat? How could he not have realized that?

He stepped toward her. "You're cold. I shouldn't have dragged you out here. I just didn't like the way we left things at the store."

"I didn't either. I'm sorry I can't fill in more of the blanks for you," she said as he walked her to her car.

"Oh, but you have helped," he insisted. "You told me I was a hero. I feel a lot better," he joked.

She swatted him on the arm. Just like old times. Smiling, she climbed into her car, started the engine and drove off. When she checked her rearview mirror, he was still standing beside his SUV. She thought he was watching her leave until she realized he was on his cell phone.

Chapter Thirteen

The next morning, Deputy Montgomery drove over to Emery's bike shop. He hadn't slept well, no surprise. He'd lain awake worrying about Olivia, worrying he wasn't going to get this case solved before someone else lost his—or her—life.

He'd finally roused this morning feeling as if he was racing against a ticking time bomb. But as he swung by the shop, he found that Emery hadn't opened yet. As he drove away, he saw Krystal pull up to the shop, apparently also expecting Emery to be at work. She pulled in, saw that the shop was closed and took off again as if in a hurry.

Curious as to why she was looking for Emery and why in such a rush, he turned around and followed her. When she made her way into Emery's apartment house parking lot, he stopped up the block and waited.

She seemed in an awful rush to speak to Emery. Had something happened? What could be so important that she had to see him this morning?

He warned himself, as he got out of his patrol SUV, that it might not have anything to do with his case. All his instincts, though, told him that there was a lot more going on with Olivia's old gang than it appeared. He couldn't shake the feeling that they all might have been in on it.

Jaden heard Krystal's raised voice even before he reached Emery's apartment at the back of the complex. He stood outside the apartment door for a moment, catching only snatches of the argument since she seemed to be the only one speaking and apparently moving around in an agitated state.

He knocked lightly, not surprised the occupants hadn't heard. Then he tried the knob. It turned in his hand and the door swung open. The apartment was small, cluttered, and smelled of stale pizza and beer. He stopped just inside the door where he could hear what was being said deeper in the apartment.

"You have to protect me," Krystal was saying. "I didn't want any part of this, and you know it." He couldn't hear Emery's reply. "This wasn't supposed to happen." She sounded close to tears. "Are you listening to me?"

Something hit the floor and shattered. Emery swore, and chair legs scraped across the flooring before there was another crash and his voice rose in anger. "Knock it off! Or so help me…"

From the kitchen doorway, Jaden saw a knocked-over chair and what appeared to be spilled coffee next to a shattered cup on the floor. Emery had Krystal backed up against the kitchen counter, his hands on her shoulders. He was saying, "Keep it together. Stop panicking. No one is going to find out unless you keep opening your big mouth." He shook her so hard, she banged her head against the kitchen cabinet.

"I hope I'm not interrupting anything," the deputy said, stepping into the kitchen.

Emery immediately let go of Krystal and moved back, his boots crunching on the broken glass glittering on the floor. Krystal moved deeper into the kitchen, her back to them as she hugged herself.

"Which one of you is going to tell me what's going on?" the deputy asked. "No one is going to find out what? How about you, Krystal? Why don't you tell me why you're panicking?"

She turned slowly, her face flushed, eyes bright with unshed tears, but from the set of her jaw, she wasn't talking now.

"We can do this here or I can take you both down to the sheriff's office."

"On what charge?" Emery demanded.

"Assault, for starters."

Neither spoke for a moment. Emery began to clean up the mess on the floor. Jaden looked at Krystal, who had recovered and now looked defiant.

Jaden pulled up a chair and sat down. "I overheard enough to know that you're both involved in what happened out at Starling on Halloween. What I want to know is what the two of you are hiding. What was the plan that night? It was your idea to go out to Starling, Emery. Planning a murder?"

Krystal's expression changed to one of alarm. "Emery?" He had finished wiping up the floor and dumped the broken cup into the trash, clearly stalling for time.

"You've got it all wrong," he said and exchanged a look with Krystal before he righted the chair and sat down. "We were just going to play a prank. That's all it was supposed to be. Just scare some people."

So, Krystal had been in on it. Jaden turned to her. "How did you get to Starling without anyone noticing?"

When she didn't answer, Emery did for her. "She hid in the back of my van. With all the junk back there, no one was the wiser."

"Weren't Dean and Jenny still down where you parked?" Jaden asked.

There was pride in her voice when Krystal finally joined in. "They were busy arguing, so they didn't notice when I opened the back and climbed out."

"What was the plan?" the deputy asked.

"She was dressed in all black, her hood up, and wearing a big, floppy dark hat," Emery said. "Anyone who saw her would think they were seeing—"

"Elden Rusk," Jaden said with a nod. "You said you wanted to scare *some* people? Cody and Olivia?" He looked at Krystal, then shifted his gaze to Emery when neither spoke. "Rob and the girls you were with? What about Dean and Jenny?" When neither answered, he said, "Who was it you really wanted to scare?" He watched the two exchange another look. "Rob Perkins," he guessed. "Why?"

Emery looked away for a moment, as if making up his mind, then said, "He owed me money. He promised to pay before he left town, but I didn't believe him. I knew that once he was gone, I'd never see a penny of it. All his big talk about his condo and his new job out there in Seattle..." He shook his head. "I didn't believe a word of it."

"Why would he lie?"

"Because it wasn't just me he owed money to," Emery said. "He'd gotten involved with the wrong people."

Jaden groaned inwardly, thinking this would have been nice to know from the get-go. "The wrong people? Drug people?"

Emery shrugged. "I just knew that he needed to get out of town. He said he wasn't planning to leave until after Saturday. But I found out that he'd already packed his truck in his garage and was planning to take off Halloween night. That's why he'd wanted to go out to Starling in my van.

He hates my driving, so I knew something was up. I texted Krystal to check his house and garage."

"I looked through a crack in the blinds into his bedroom," she said. "The closets were empty, the bureau drawers dropped out on the bed and almost everything taken. I checked the garage, and just like Emery suspected, Rob was planning a quick getaway."

"He was going to miss the going-away party I was throwing for him Saturday night," Emery said bitterly. "Where he promised to pay me what he owed me with interest. Lying piece of—"

"So, the two of you decided to kill him," Jaden said, making Emery start.

"No! Not that I didn't want to, but…" He shook his head. "It's just money, right? He saved my life once. Sure, I was pissed, but I couldn't kill him. What would be the point? It wouldn't get my money back." He shrugged. "I just wanted him to think that Elden Rusk had come for him that night. My going-away present for the bastard."

Did Jaden believe Emery was telling the truth, that he'd just wanted to scare Rob by resurrecting Elden Rusk? After all, it had been Emery's idea to go out to Starling on Halloween night. Rob must have gone along with it because it would have been suspicious if he hadn't.

The deputy looked to Krystal, who was still standing at the other end of the table, her back to the wall. What was in it for her? "What did he owe you, Krystal?"

She seemed surprised by the question but recovered quickly. "Do I look like I had money to give him?" Her laugh didn't quite ring true.

"It wasn't money he wanted from you," Jaden said. "But he owed you something, didn't he?"

She chewed on her lower lip, her eyes shiny as she looked away.

"He'd promised to take her with him when he left," Emery said, getting an evil-eye glare from Krystal.

"But once you saw his loaded pickup, you knew different," Jaden said. He felt for her but wondered what that kind of humiliation could stir up in her. He recalled her chasing Livie out of town. Would she have run her off the road if she hadn't gone in the ditch?

"You were hiding in the back of the van when Rob and Emery picked up those underage girls Halloween night," Jaden said as he tried to work it out. "That had to make you angry. Angry enough that when you saw your chance, you took it?" But was she strong enough to push a concrete wall over on Rob? Only if Emery had helped her.

"Why would I care about Rob?" Krystal said. "I was with Cody. I never really believed Rob was serious."

"Only, Cody was with his old girlfriend down in a root cellar," Jaden said, trying to imagine how yet another betrayal that night could have been the straw that broke the camel's back. "You saw Olivia climb out and leave him to go for help. Save him or... You had to be furious by then. No one could blame you for picking up a rock and hurling it down at him. You just wanted him to hurt like he had made you. You didn't mean to almost kill him."

A tear escaped and ran down her cheek. She lifted her gaze to meet his. "I couldn't hurt Cody. I love him and he loves me," she said, making Emery look over at her in surprise. "It wasn't me. When you found him, wasn't Olivia the one standing over him? Maybe you should ask her what happened."

"Did you see anyone else?" the deputy asked, tending to believe at least part of her story. She shook her head.

He thought she could have wanted to scare Cody, but he doubted she'd intended to put him in the hospital, let alone kill him. That was, if she had been the one to injure him.

Rising from the table, Jaden thought back to the argument he'd overheard before coming into the apartment. "Any idea why Rob had insisted you all stay until midnight?"

"I didn't know then, but I do now," Emery said and swore. "He was killing time with us, using his old friends to shield him from the scary people he owed money to. Then, after midnight, he was skipping town."

"You know that for a fact?" Jaden asked, even though it certainly appeared that way.

Emery shook his head. But if right, Rob was leaving in the dead of night, running from debts and deceits, maybe even running for his life.

"Who are these scary people?" he asked Krystal.

"I heard him on the phone with them once," she said after exchanging a look with Emery. "It sounded like they would be crossing the border the next day. From what I could tell, they were threatening him. After he hung up, he went in the bathroom and threw up. I didn't ask."

"It had to be drugs," Emery said, pushing that theory. "I know he made a lot of trips up to the border." It was only sixty-five miles from Libby to the Canadian border, nothing to drive when you lived in a state as large as Montana.

"You never asked him why he made so many trips to the border?" the deputy asked.

Emery shook his head. "He told me he had a girlfriend up there. I knew he was lying. But, like Krystal, I didn't ask. I wanted nothing to do with it."

OLIVIA HAD SPENT all morning trying to shake off the terrifying dream she'd had the night before.

She'd been back out at Starling. Only, this time, Cody had climbed out of the root cellar first, leaving her to die. She'd screamed for help until her throat was raw before a dark shadow had fallen over her. She'd looked up and Elden Rusk had been peering down at her. But then she'd seen who'd been standing next to Rusk and she'd gasped. Cody, smiling down at her, a rock in his hand.

She told herself it had just been a bad dream. It didn't mean anything. It didn't even make sense. Yet she found herself worrying about Cody. That really made no sense, given that she'd been the one in the hole, the one in danger, not Cody.

Still, she called his number. She'd tell him about the dream. They'd laugh about it. She'd put it behind her. His phone rang four times before voicemail picked up.

"You've reached Cody Ryan. Leave a message."

Olivia hesitated as she heard the beep. "Cody, it's Olivia. I had this crazy dream last night. I just wanted to make sure you were all right." She recalled their talk the evening before by the river, his need to remember what had happened Halloween night. He wouldn't go out to Starling, thinking it might help him remember, would he? "Please call me."

After she disconnected, she was more convinced than ever that he might have gone out there this morning. Hadn't people in the area been warned to stay away? Been told how dangerous it was because of all the debris left by the tornado? Like that would stop Cody.

She paused only a moment before she called the deputy. He picked up at once. Just the sound of his voice steadied her. He'd always had that effect on her. "Is the crime team done out at Starling?"

He instantly sounded suspicious. "Why are you asking me that?"

"Cody is determined to remember who attacked him. I couldn't reach him this morning. I think he might go out there."

Jaden swore. "Don't you go out there," he ordered, making her bristle.

"I didn't say I was going out there."

"It would be just like you. Do I have to remind you that there is still a killer on the loose, not to mention how dangerous it is out there?"

She was sorry she'd called him and said as much before disconnecting.

"That man knows you," her mother said from her bedroom doorway. "You're thinking about going to Starling because of that boy."

"Neither of you know me," Olivia snapped. "But it doesn't stop either of you from telling me what to do. Cody is my *friend*. He's hurting right now. I had this dream last night…" She waved a hand through the air. "I wouldn't expect either of you to understand."

Her mother just shook her head, turned around and disappeared back into the kitchen. Olivia could smell bacon cooking, which she realized was probably why her mother had come to her room, to offer her breakfast.

In the kitchen, she hugged her mom with one arm and said, "I'd love some bacon. Oh, and pancakes too? You're spoiling me." When her mother didn't respond, she added, "I'm sorry. I worry about my friends. Cody isn't doing very well right now."

"Cody's a big boy. He can take care of himself." Her mother plated bacon and pancakes and turned to hand it

to her. "You chasin' after him sends mixed signals to the deputy—the one you say you're in love with."

"I'm not chasing after Cody. I need this whole investigation over. If Jaden and I stand any chance, I can't be one of the suspects."

Her mother shook her head. "Listen to your mother for a change and let the man do his job. In the meantime, stay away from Cody Ryan."

JADEN HAD BEEN about to go inside Rob Perkins's house when Livie had called. He swore. She wouldn't go out to Starling looking for Cody, would she?

Probably, he thought with another curse. He used Perkins's keys to open the front door of the house. Just as Emery had described to Olivia, the place had been cleaned out. Only worn furniture remained and not a lot of that. In the bedroom, he saw the mess the man had left. Perkins had been in a hurry—just as Emery had thought.

Once Jaden stepped into the garage and saw the packed pickup, he had to agree. Definitely a man on the run. Perkins was leaving town.

He pulled on latex gloves and opened the passenger side of the vehicle. The first thing he saw was the automatic rifle wedged into the space between the seats. The serial number had been ground off. In the glove box, he found a handgun and ammunition. At the back of the space, he found an envelope stuffed with hundred-dollar bills.

Closing the glove box compartment, Jaden took a look in the backpack on the passenger seat. Another handgun. More ammunition. In a side pocket, more money. Zipping the pocket up, he closed the door and took a look in the back, not surprised to find more weapons and boxes of ammunition, as if expecting World War III.

Closing the door, he made the call to have the pickup taken into evidence by one of the state boys in the area. All his instincts told him this was bigger than some old friends getting in a drunken argument and one of them ending up dead and another injured.

He called Sheriff Brandt Parker and updated his boss on the investigation, even though there wasn't much to tell. Then he called DCI and requested help to find out if Rob Perkins had a job in Seattle or not. "He'd allegedly purchased a condo out there and was going to work for a tech firm. From what I can tell, the man didn't even own a computer."

After hanging up, he locked the house and garage and waited for a state highway patrolman to arrive and secure the property until the pickup could be moved and the house processed.

He felt anxious, angry that all he could think about was Livie. She was just fool enough to go out to Starling. He tried Cody's number. It went to voicemail. He didn't leave a message. What could the man hope to find out there? All the evidence taken by the state boys had been bagged. Or was there another reason Cody had told Olivia he'd wanted to go back out there?

Either way, Jaden had no choice but to go back to that place he'd hoped to never see again.

On the way out to Starling, he got a call from the coroner. The autopsy results were pretty much as expected. But given what the deputy had since learned about Rob Perkins, he was surprised that the man had had no drugs in his system. There was also no indication that he was a drug user.

That didn't mean he hadn't been involved in the selling end. Still, it seemed unusual. But then, where had Perkins gotten all that money he'd had in his pickup? And why all the guns and ammunition? He was involved in something suspect, no doubt about that, and it had probably gotten him killed.

Ahead, Jaden could see the turnoff to Starling and began to slow. He told himself this was a wild-goose chase, driving out here. He had better things to do than chase down his ex-fiancée. It bothered him that she was so worried about Cody. She'd said they weren't together. All indications were that Cody was now dating Krystal. Maybe they were just friends, as Livie'd kept saying. Jaden knew how she could be like a mama bear with her friends who were in trouble. He'd seen that in college.

What was left of Starling loomed ahead. He hadn't been out here since Halloween night. Driving up the road, he caught glimpses of the damage the tornado had done. Only a few structures remained standing against the skyline.

As he came over a rise, he saw Livie's vehicle and swore. Hadn't he known? He sighed as he pulled up next to her, cut his engine and got out. She had come alone, hadn't she? Cody Ryan wasn't with her, was he?

That was when he saw her trudging up the hill, avoiding the debris. He knew at once where she was headed and hurried after her. The dirt around the open root cellar was unstable. He hated to think what could happen to her.

He just hoped to get to her first. "Olivia!" he called. "Livie!"

OLIVIA STOPPED AND turned at the sound of her nickname. Jaden was the only one who called her that. Just the sound of it sent her heart pounding.

She saw him climbing up the hillside toward her. When she'd gotten here and seen all the destruction—and no Cody—she'd almost turned around and left. She couldn't imagine there was anything to find. Yet she understood why Cody might want to come back out here. It had been so dark and frightening Halloween night down in that hole with the house that had been over them ripped away.

Now, in broad daylight, she wanted to see it and possibly get a different perspective. She knew it had something to do with her nightmare that had made her start up the hillside. The wind had been blowing, so she hadn't heard a vehicle approaching. She'd only stopped when she'd heard Jaden call her "Livie."

As he approached, winding a path through the destruction, she could tell he wasn't happy with her. Yet she was glad to see him. Even in bright sunshine, this place gave her the willies. Even almost completely destroyed.

Jaden said nothing at first when he reached her. He only looked at her before shaking his head. "What are you doing, Livie?" His voice was soft, caring, maybe even loving.

"Looking for answers," she said over the wind that whipped her hair. She started to brush it back, but Jaden was already reaching. He caught an errant lock and held it between his fingers. "You called me 'Livie.'"

He nodded as he tucked the errant lock of hair behind her ear. His hand seemed to move of its own accord to the nape of her neck. He dug his fingers deeper into her hair as he drew her closer. "What am I going to do with you?"

She shook her head. She couldn't speak. She could barely breathe. She looked into his eyes and saw desire burning there. He wanted her as much as she wanted him.

For a moment, she feared that he would draw away, release his hold on her and not go through with the kiss. She ached to feel his lips on hers. She could see him fighting a battle within himself. If he kissed her, he could no longer deny how he felt about her, about them.

The wind shrieked around them, whirling dust and dirt. She'd never felt more alone with him, as if they were the only two people left on earth, than she did in this moment. He pulled her closer. She leaned into him as they both fought the wind on the hillside, their lips only a breath away from touching.

"Livie," he said, making her pulse spike, and then his mouth was on hers with an unbridled passion that made her weak with longing. He wrapped an arm around her, holding her up as the kiss deepened, and there was nothing but the two of them and their longing for each other.

Neither of them heard the sound of a vehicle approach, then turn around and leave. The wind was too loud, even if they hadn't been so lost in each other.

Chapter Fourteen

Shaken to his boots, Jaden drew back from the kiss. This was exactly what he hadn't meant to do. Yet he couldn't regret it as he looked in Livie's eyes. "We can't do this. I'm in the middle of an investigation and you're—"

"Still a suspect."

He nodded and tipped in to touch his forehead to hers for a moment before stepping back. "What are you doing out here? Cody's not here, is he?"

She shook her head. "I had this bad dream last night. It was so dark that night… I wanted to see the root cellar in daylight. I don't know what I'm hoping to find. Answers. Reassurance. Something, since I haven't been able to forget being in that hole and then seeing Cody lying down there." Her gaze locked with his again. "And seeing the doubt on your face, I didn't want you to suspect me anymore."

"I don't want to, either, but you know we can't take this any further until this investigation is over. That's if it's something we want to do."

"How can you even ask after that kiss?" she demanded. "I never stopped loving you. It's why I came back."

He hated to ask, especially after that kiss. "What about Cody?"

"Cody and I are just friends."

"Does he know that?" Jaden heard himself ask and wanted to kick himself.

"Yes, Cody knows that. We grew up together, shared a lot of things, but all we've ever really been is good friends. He'd thought we'd end up together and was upset when I left town, but he knows better now."

He knew she had a strong connection to Cody. Wasn't that the reason he'd called off the engagement? Livie had years of memories with Cody, something Jaden didn't have with her. Maybe what he'd picked up on was her longing for Montana and home more than her old high school boyfriend.

While he'd wanted to hear her say it, the kiss had convinced him even more than her words. She was right. Once his lips had touched hers, he'd felt his doubts dissolve and blow away like smoke on the breeze.

"If you're determined to see the root cellar..." He motioned toward the hillside. "Let me make sure it's safe to go over there."

OLIVIA GLADLY LET Jaden lead the way through the debris. They had to skirt around houses torn off their foundations and dropped at random on the hillside. Everywhere there were piles of lumber and pieces of twisted metal to traverse.

They hadn't gone far, though, when Jaden stopped to wait for her. She quickly caught up after finding herself gawking at the awesome power of what had been a small tornado by national standards. She saw that he was standing next to the hole in the ground.

"Don't get too close," he warned. "It's caved in some more."

The root cellar looked so much larger than it had seemed that night, even with more dirt having fallen in. She shivered, remembering being down there when the tornado hit, feeling it trying to suck them up and carry them away.

"Are you all right?" Jaden asked. The wind had picked up to a low howl, much like it had Halloween night before the real storm hit.

Pushing her hair back from her face, she looked down. "It doesn't seem as deep now," she said as her dream came back to her. In the dream, when she'd looked up and seen Cody standing over her, the hole had been so much deeper, so much more frightening.

"Have you seen enough?"

She glanced around and nodded. If Cody did come out here, she couldn't imagine that he would find any more answers than she had. "I'm done."

JADEN FOLLOWED LIVIE back to her turnoff to home. They'd stopped earlier when they'd reached their vehicles but kept their distance. He knew it wouldn't take a lot for him to cross the line with her during this investigation. He hadn't realized how much he'd missed her, how much he wanted her, that no matter what happened, he would always want her.

The kiss had sealed it. He felt even more determined to solve this case so he and Livie could see what happened next. He believed her about Cody Ryan. But he wondered if Cody had accepted that she'd moved on.

It all came back to Rob Perkins, he realized as he forced himself to concentrate on the case. Whatever Perkins had been up to, Jaden couldn't believe that his friends hadn't known, might even have been involved. He called the hospital, only to find out that Dean Marsh had been released.

He'd only just disconnected when he got a call from the Fortune Creek dispatcher. Dean Marsh had been trying to reach him. "He sounded upset and said he needed to talk to you right away."

On the outskirts of town, Jaden decided to swing by Dean's house, hoping to catch him at home. He doubted Dean would have returned to his job in construction yet, especially with a broken arm. He hit pay dirt when he saw Dean's car in the driveway. The vehicle had taken a beating during the tornado but apparently still ran after being brought into town when the state boys had finished with it.

Dean must have heard him coming up the steps, because he opened the door before the deputy could knock. "Thanks for coming by." He motioned Jaden inside. "I don't know if this is important," he said once they were seated in the living room, "but I overheard my wife on the phone planning to meet someone after Halloween. She didn't leave me because of what me and Jenny had going on. Apparently, she'd been planning this for some time."

Jaden had to admit he'd been surprised at how quickly Angie had bailed on the marriage—even before they'd known what had happened to her husband. "You have any idea who she was meeting?"

"No, but I got a call asking if I had made a reservation for a hotel in Spokane, Washington. I hadn't. The reservation had been made *two weeks ago*. Apparently, Angie hadn't checked in when she was supposed to—the night after Halloween—and she hadn't called to cancel, so they were going to have to charge me for the first night as per their policy. It was for a room with a king-size bed. Angie had told them there would be two people."

"Have you heard from your wife, Dean?" Jaden asked.

He shook his head. "I don't blame her for running off with someone, but I'm worried about her. Why hadn't she checked in? What if something has happened to her?"

"You should consult a lawyer," the deputy advised. "You might want to cancel your credit cards. That way, you'll probably be hearing from her. Let me know when you do."

"Can't you put out a BOLO on her car? Something. I just need to know she's all right."

Jaden hesitated. "I can do that. One more thing. Some of Rob's friends seem to think he might have been involved with the wrong people. Would you know anything about that?"

"Wrong people?"

"Drug dealers," Jaden said.

Dean blinked. "Rob? Seriously?" He sounded genuinely surprised.

"I can't seem to find anywhere he was employed for the past few years," Jaden said.

"He was working with Angie."

"Doing what?"

"She has a craft business she's been running out of an old barn in the country. Buys furniture and redoes it. Rob was helping her."

"Was it profitable?" Jaden asked.

"Seemed to be, but she wasn't paying enough taxes, you know?"

The deputy thought he did. "Where is this barn?"

Chapter Fifteen

"You're acting strange. Is it because I asked you to help me with the jelly?"

Olivia looked at her mother sitting across from her at the table. Each year, Sharon Brooks picked the crab apples from the huge trees in the backyard and froze the juice to make jelly once the weather got colder.

"I already told you that I'd be happy to help with the jelly."

"You're sure?" Her mother had insisted on making her lunch when she'd returned to the house. Beanie weenies, her mother's specialty.

"If I'm acting strangely, it's because I had an odd morning," she said, her gaze on the last few bites of her lunch. She could feel her mother waiting. Eventually, the woman would get it out of her. "I went out to Starling."

"Why would you do that?" Sharon demanded, making her wish she hadn't told her.

"I wanted to see the root cellar where we were trapped during the tornado." She shrugged. "I had a nightmare about it."

"I can't believe you'd go out there again and alone. What were you thinking?"

"I didn't go alone. Jaden followed me out there. He made

sure it was safe." She could feel her mother's eyes on her. The woman knew her too well. "He kissed me." She smiled and felt her face light up. "It was…amazing."

"I guess that answers all your doubts," her mother said and rose from the table to start clearing away the dishes.

"He's the one who had doubts," Olivia corrected her, only to have her mother huff. "I love Jaden. I want to marry him."

"And how does he feel about it?" her mother asked, turning to look at her daughter. "This kiss have the same effect on him?"

"Yes, I think so."

"You think so." She turned back to her dishes. "You think you're ready to marry a deputy sheriff and live in Fortune Creek, huh. What about Cody?"

"I told you. He's just a friend."

Her mother kept hand-washing the dishes in the sink.

Olivia rose to carry her dishes over. "Why don't you let me do that?" With a shock, she realized that her mother was crying.

"Mother?" No response. "Mom, what is it?"

Shaking the water off her hands, her mother reached for the dish towel and dried her hands before she looked at her. "Will I see more of you if you're living closer?"

"Yes, of course." She saw how much she'd hurt her mother the years she'd stayed away. "I'm so sorry that I didn't come home. It wasn't you." She reached out and her mother stepped into her arms. She held her close as her mom cried, reminded of all the times her mother had held her when she was growing up. It had just been the two of them. They'd been close. She hated how much she'd hurt her mother.

Her cell phone rang from where she'd left it on the table. She ignored it.

"You should get that," Sharon said, stepping from her arms to reach for a paper towel to wipe her face. "It might be important. Go ahead."

Olivia picked up the phone, saw it was Cody and hesitated. Turning around, she saw that her mother was busy finishing up the dishes. "I need to take this," she said and stepped into the other room. "Hello?"

JADEN DROVE OUT of town on a road with no traffic, toward the mountains. Dean had said the barn where his wife and Rob worked together was out there.

He hadn't been driving long before a barn shape appeared ahead. The structure was small by barn standards, more like a large shed and surrounded by a barbed-wire fence. As he pulled off the road, stopping at the barbed-wire gate, he climbed out. He'd opened his share of Montana ranch gates. Shoving it aside, he drove in, pretty sure of what he was going to find.

The door to the small barn-shaped building had a large padlock on it. Jaden walked around the side to look for a window. He found one covered with what appeared to be black tar paper. Angie really didn't want anyone to see what she was working on with Rob, he thought as he circled the building to find all the windows blacked out.

Walking to his patrol SUV, he opened the rear and dug out what he needed from the tools he carried. Hesitating, he pulled out his phone and called Judge Nicholas Grand back upstate. "I'm going to need a warrant," he said.

"Heard you were working on a murder investigation down there."

"I'm pretty sure I'm about to find out why the victim was killed. But it means getting into a structure where he worked. The owner has left town in a rush."

The judge chuckled. "Could be a body in that structure. Who knows what you'll find. You'll get your warrant."

"Thanks, Judge." He disconnected, picked up his hacksaw and headed for the front door again. It took a few minutes to cut through the padlock. Leaning his hacksaw against the outside of the building, he started to open the door but stopped. He knew that if he was right, the place could be booby-trapped.

Picking up the saw again, he stepped back and pushed the door open with the blade end. Nothing happened. He looked past the doorway into the room, seeing pretty much what he'd expected. Several large tables. Scales. Baggies.

Dean had said that Angie had been restoring old furniture. *Restoring* didn't seem to be the right word. The old furniture was clearly being used to hide bagged drugs.

As he reached to close the door, he brushed something inside the room. An alarm went off. He slammed the door, the alarm still blaring—not that there was anyone around to hear it. Had the alarm been to scare people away?

Frowning, he shook his head. No. It had been to warn someone that the door had been breached. If he had worked here, he would know how to turn it off—or never set it off in the first place.

As he pulled out his phone to alert the DEA state boys, he wondered if the alarm was also set up to notify whoever was in charge of the operation. Angie? She apparently was long gone. Rob wasn't being notified of the alarm. Clearly, someone else was involved in the operation.

WHEN THERE WAS no response on the other end of the phone line, Olivia asked, "Cody? Are you there?" She was beginning to wonder if he'd accidentally called her.

"Sorry, I had a customer," he said. She could hear the

could hear the hardware store music in the background. "Cody?" The phone went silent.

For a moment, she almost called him back and told him she'd go to Starling with him. He'd sounded so sad. But then the front door opened.

Her mother asked, "Is everything all right?"

Pocketing her phone, she turned and smiled. "Just getting ready to make some crab apple jelly with my mother. Just like old times. I need to start paying more attention to how it's done. Who knows—one of these days I might have a kitchen of my own. Though no one makes jelly as good as yours."

Her mother smiled and said, "You and your malarkey," but Olivia could tell that she was touched by the compliment as they both headed for the kitchen.

OUTSIDE TOWN, at the barn, Jaden pulled his coat tighter around him as he waited for the state DEA team to arrive. This case had been running them ragged. Knowing that Rob Perkins had been involved in this drug distribution business might be the key to solving his murder.

Rob could have been involved with dangerous people, as Emery had suggested. The question was, were they his friends? He thought about Dean. How could he not know what his wife and Rob were involved in? And if he had known, had Dean just thrown his wife under the bus to save himself?

His cell phone rang. Angie Marsh's car had been found in Spokane, abandoned on the street. "Looks like it's been looted," the police officer told him.

"Any sign of Angie Marsh?"

"Checked the surveillance camera in the area." He described the woman who'd gotten out of the car. Petite, dark-haired, wearing jeans and a hoodie. It hadn't captured much of her face, but she was young.

That definitely sounded like Angie. The officer said he would get back to Jaden if he had anything to report about the woman. Like if her body was found. Or if another camera picked her up getting into someone's vehicle.

He thanked the officer and disconnected as a gust of wind out of the nearby mountains sent a chill through the air. What was it about this case? He felt as if he wasn't getting anywhere. It didn't help that Livie might be more involved than she realized.

Jaden squinted as dust blew past, reminding him of the hillside at Starling. Everything reminded him of Livie.

That thought didn't get a chance to go any further as he saw a van drive slowly by on the road, then speed up and disappear over the rise. He hadn't needed to see the van's license plate or to see him behind the wheel to know that it was Emery's gray van. What had he been doing out there, on this particular road, so far away from town?

The alarm. More than likely it was to warn those involved that someone had found out their secret—or already knew their secret and had come hoping to find drugs. Either way, whoever was running this operation now knew.

He waited, wondering if Emery would return this way. Not if he was guilty, in which case, he'd take another way back to town.

Even after the DEA boys arrived, Jaden kept an eye on the road.

The van hadn't come back.

Chapter Sixteen

Jaden wasn't surprised when he went to the bike shop and found it closed. No sign of Emery. He drove by his apartment. No van parked in the lot. No answer at Emery's apartment door. On impulse, he headed for Krystal's.

Still no sign of the van, but Cody's rig was parked next to Krystal's and the curtains were drawn in the living room window. He didn't bother to stop.

After driving around town and still not finding Emery or his van, Jaden thought about heading back out to the barn. But the state crew was still there processing the place. He told himself that Emery might have just been curious when he'd driven past earlier to see if the deputy had taken him up on checking it out.

What Jaden really wanted to do was to drive out and check on Livie. He felt antsy, like he always did when an investigation started coming together. It was the most dangerous time in any case, but especially in a murder investigation. He was getting close. Someone was getting nervous.

He pulled out his phone, opting to text Livie instead of showing up at her door.

You OK?

Making crab apple jelly with my mom.

My favorite, he texted back.

I remember. I'll save you a couple of jars!

Great. Tell your mom thank you.

At loose ends, he checked in with his boss in Fortune Creek, then drove down to the café. His growling stomach reminded him that he hadn't had anything since lunch.

Just the thought of Sharon Brooks's crab apple jelly had made him hungry. He thought about that one late night back in college when he and Livie had gotten into a care package her mom had sent. There was a jar of the jelly and peanut butter, along with homemade bread. He smiled at the memory. Best jelly he'd ever tasted.

Taking a seat in a booth facing the street, Jaden watched the sparse traffic as he waited for his meal order. This time of year, off season, things were usually quiet. He thought about everything he'd learned so far on the case. He had a pretty good idea why Rob Perkins had been killed. But it weighed on him that, while he had suspects, he still wasn't close to arresting the person who had committed the murder or the person who had assaulted Cody. Were they the same one?

His food came and he dug in, reminding himself that he'd solved one old murder at Starling, though, thanks to Rusk. He recalled the male remains. Make those two murders. Remembering that Evangeline might have still been pregnant, he amended the thought. Make those three murders. Solved, but he would never be able to prove it, let alone get justice. Or maybe Elden Rusk had already gotten justice since he was trapped in his own guilt until he died.

As Jaden was leaving the café, he spotted Emery driving by in his van. Once in his patrol SUV, he sped after him. He started to hit his lights and siren, but realized Emery was headed to his apartment. He followed, parking next to him in the lot.

Emery didn't seem happy to see him as Jaden climbed out and approached the van. The man's scared expression gave him hope that Emery was ready to tell him the truth.

"WOULD YOU MIND if I took a couple of jars of jelly to share?" Olivia asked her mother. She'd been antsy after they'd completed their work. She needed fresh air. Mostly, she wanted an excuse to see Jaden.

Sharon Brooks sighed. "Is there a handsome deputy on your list?"

Olivia grinned. "There is." She told her mother about that night back in college when they'd opened her care package. At least, she told her the PG part. "He loved it. Said it was his favorite."

"You won't be late?" her mother asked, looking outside. It got dark earlier and earlier this time of year. The wind whistled through the bare branches of the trees. One limb scraped against the side of the house. "Something's blowing in," she warned. "Hate to see you get caught in a snowstorm."

"I'll be back long before that," she promised and loaded a couple of jars into her bag, thinking she'd drop one off at the hardware store before it closed.

"Thanks for helping with the jelly," her mother said as Olivia started for the door.

"It was fun," she called over her shoulder and was out

the door, headed for her car. It had been fun making the jelly with her mother. She remembered the two of them working in the kitchen together when she was a girl. Her mother had sewn her a small apron to wear. She'd been so proud of it, she thought now as she swallowed the lump that rose in her throat.

Climbing behind the wheel, she hesitated as she looked back at the house. She could see the flicker of the television screen, the silhouette of her mother curled up in her chair to watch her stories. Olivia told herself that she wouldn't be gone that long. Maybe the two of them could watch a movie together when she got back.

That decided, she headed toward town, hoping to get there before the hardware store closed. Then she planned to go by the grocery store to pick up some peanut butter and bread before going to Jaden's motel. She knew it was risky. He might turn her away. Or even more risky, he might invite her in.

The jelly was just an excuse. He would realize that right away. Hopefully, he'd hear her out. She needed to tell him she wasn't leaving Montana. That she'd quit her job in California before she'd come home. That she loved him and was through running away—from being terrified that she would end up with her mother's life.

The lights were still on at the hardware store as she parked and, taking one of the jars of jelly, headed for the front door. The bell tinkled as the door closed behind her. She saw that some of the lights had already been turned off, but the music was still playing softly, so she knew someone was still there.

"Hello!" she called as she headed toward the back, where the office was. "Jelly delivery!" No answer. Her footsteps echoed on the worn wood floor as she moved deeper into the building.

The lights were on in the office, but she didn't see anyone. She caught a gust of wind coming down the hallway from the open back door to the alley. "Cody?"

"I THINK WE should talk," Jaden said as Emery climbed out of the van with obvious reluctance.

"I've had a rotten day, Deputy," the bike shop owner said. "Can't we do this in the morning?"

"I'm afraid not. We can talk in your apartment or go for a ride in my patrol car. Up to you."

Emery raked a hand through his hair. "I guess it's my apartment, then." He started in that direction, walking as if he had the weight of the world on his shoulders. Jaden suspected he did.

Once inside the apartment, Emery headed straight for the refrigerator, opening it and pulling out a beer. "Wanna join me?" When Jaden declined, he popped it open and chugged half of the can. Wiping his mouth, he said, "Let's get this over with. What do you want?"

"Why did you drive by the barn earlier in your van?"

Emery frowned. "What barn?"

"The one Rob and Angie worked out of." He saw the man tense.

"Sorry, but I have no idea what you're talking about."

"Are you saying you don't know what barn I'm talking about or that you didn't drive past earlier?" Jaden asked.

"Angie's restored furniture business? Yeah, I know where it is, but I didn't drive by it today. I didn't even have my van until an hour ago."

"Who had it?"

Emery finished the can of beer and, with a loud burp,

tossed the can in the direction of the trash. His aim was off. The can hit the wall and clattered to the floor. He ignored it and reached for another beer. He took his time opening it before he looked up. "This is a small town. We're like family here."

Jaden saw the pain in his face. "I know it's a small town. Hell, all of Montana is a small town. I understand local loyalty, but this is more than covering for a friend. This is murder and drugs."

Emery walked over to the secondhand-looking couch and dropped onto it. He cradled the beer in his large hands, his head down.

"Who had your van earlier? You know I'm going to find out. Are you covering for this person because you're also involved in the drug business or—"

"I had nothing to do with it. From the get-go, I told them to keep me out of it. I've got my bike business. That's all I need, all I want." He stared down at the beer for a moment before he said, "Cody borrowed my van. He said he had some things he needed to haul." He took a drink. When he looked up, there were tears in his eyes.

"I know Angie and Rob were involved in the drug business," Jaden said. "How is Cody involved?" Emery shook his head. "If you withhold what you know, it makes you an accessory. He just used your van and I suspect it wasn't the first time."

Emery dropped his head again. "I told you. I didn't want to be involved. I didn't ask. But Cody's been desperate to get out of that hardware store. He's worked there since he was a kid. His old man told him that if he left him to run it by himself, he'd sell it and wouldn't give him a dime. Cody had to stay, but he was at the point that he'd do *anything* to get out from under his father's thumb."

Jaden wondered how close Cody was getting to breaking free of his father, the hardware store and this town. "You told me that Rob owed a lot of people money," the deputy said as he took a chair across from Emery. "Did he owe Cody?" He took the man's silence as a yes. "How desperate was Cody? Was he desperate enough to murder Rob?"

The answer was written all over Emery's face, even as he refused to believe it. "Cody couldn't have killed him. He was trapped down in that root cellar. Someone attacked him. It had to be the dangerous people Rob did business with."

Some of those "dangerous people" appeared to be locals, including Cody, the deputy thought. But Emery had a point. How could Cody kill Rob? He would have had to find a way out of the root-cellar hole, find Rob, kill him and climb back into the hole and get seriously injured so he still had an alibi.

Yet something Livie had said earlier teased at his memory. Something about the root-cellar hole.

OLIVIA WAS HALFWAY down the hallway past the office when she heard voices in the alley. It sounded like boxes were being loaded in a vehicle. Cody or his father must have had a late order to fill. She started to turn back, thinking she would just leave the jar of jelly on the desk in the office. She was anxious to see Jaden. Her heart filled at the thought of their earlier kiss.

Before she could reach the office, she heard Cody's voice. "Olivia?" There was a tension in it that made her turn to look toward the dark alley and the man standing in the doorway. "What are you doing here?"

She held up the jar of jelly. "I was just dropping this off

as promised. I was about to leave it on the desk in the office."

"How long have you been standing there?" he asked as he moved toward her.

"Just a few minutes. I could hear that you were busy. I didn't want to bother you." Why was he looking at her like that?

He glanced at the jelly, then at her. He seemed jumpy. "I was going to call you," he said, still moving toward her. She fought the urge to take a step back. This was Cody, the boy she'd grown up with, her first real boyfriend back in high school.

She swallowed, her throat suddenly dry. Cody had left the back door of the shop open. She could feel the chill of the wind along the hallway as if it were a funnel. "Why were you going to call me?"

He reached her, stopping just inches away, his eyes dark in the dim light, his expression reminding her of Halloween night when they'd argued. From the alley, an engine started up, then another one, both pulling slowly away. She could see that the back of each pickup was filled with boxes and shiny new equipment.

"We should take a ride," Cody said.

Olivia shook her head. "I can't. I was just—"

He grabbed her arm hard, cutting off the rest of her words. "I insist."

She tried to pull free. "Cody, you're hurting me."

He jerked her to him, his body crashing into hers. She dropped the jar of jelly. It hit and broke, the smell of crab apple jelly filling the hallway. "Don't fight me, Olivia. I don't want to hurt you, but you are coming with me—one way or the other."

"Tell me why you're acting like this," she demanded and

tried to pull away from him. She stepped into the jelly and felt herself slip, her feet sliding out from under her. Cody still had a firm grip on her arm, so he was going down with her unless he released her. He swung her around and slammed her against the wall as he struggled to stay on his feet. His grip released enough that she broke free. But as she tried to scramble away from him, he punched her, his fist connecting to the side of her head. She saw the floor come up fast to meet her as darkness closed in around her eyes.

The last thing she heard was "Damn it, Olivia. I didn't want it to end like this."

Chapter Seventeen

"Do yourself a favor," the deputy told Emery as he rose to leave. "Don't call Cody. Don't try to warn anyone involved. Unless you want to join them in prison."

"Don't worry. I'm not getting off this couch but to get another beer," the bike shop owner said. "I worried something like this would happen." He shook his head and took a gulp of his beer. "They were my friends. My brothers, man."

"I know. Any idea where I can find Cody?"

Emery hesitated, but only a moment. Maybe he was starting to realize that his friends, his brothers, had pulled him into their illegal activity knowing he didn't want to be involved. "Probably down at the hardware store. Whatever he had to move earlier is probably getting moved out the back door of the store as we speak."

Jaden left Emery on his couch and raced to the hardware store. He took the alley, hoping Emery had been right and he could catch them in the act. But the alley was empty.

The back door of the hardware store, though, was wide open.

He jumped out, weapon in hand, and moved quickly to the open doorway. His heart dropped to his boots as he caught the familiar scent of crab apple jelly.

OLIVIA BEGAN TO surface from what felt like a bottomless pitch-black pit. She became aware of movement, a blinding headache and the hum of a car engine. But what brought her out of the darkness was the memory of Cody in the alley and the realization that her wrists were bound.

She blinked, even though it hurt. Her eyes were the only thing she moved, knowing instinctively she had an advantage as long as her captor thought she was still out. She didn't have to look to her left to know who was behind the wheel. The smell of spilled crab apple jelly on her shoes brought back the memory of the hardware store hallway— and Cody.

Where was he taking her? She could hear him nervously tapping his fingers on the steering wheel. She didn't remember ever seeing him this jumpy, this…strung out? It heightened her fear—just like what she saw in the headlights. She caught glimpses of a landscape that sent her pulse pounding in her ears. This was the road to Starling. But why would he take her there?

She thought of the root cellar. The bones the tornado had uncovered. The crime scene team had finished. No one would look for her there—just as no one had thought to look for Evangeline buried down in the root cellar of an abandoned house.

"I know you're awake," Cody said with a chuckle. "You never could fool me, Olivia."

JADEN FELT TIME racing away from him as he stepped into the dimly lit hallway. He listened as he moved as soundlessly as possible. The closer he got to the front of the building, the scent of the jelly grew stronger—just like his dread and the faint sound of canned music.

Livie had been here. The realization was a scream in

his head. She'd been here and something had happened. Had she stumbled onto Cody moving product? Or robbing the place?

Pulling his flashlight out with his free hand, he flicked it on. The glow fell on something on the floor partway down the hall. Broken glass and a smear of red. Not blood, he told himself as he moved toward it.

It appeared that someone had dropped the jelly jar and then fallen? Or been dragged? His pulse thundered in his ears. Chest tight, he called out Olivia's name, even though he knew if she was there, she wasn't going to be able to answer.

He checked the building. No bodies. No Olivia. It gave him little relief, though. Where was Cody? He tried his number. It went straight to voicemail. Then he put in a call for backup.

He knew only two things. Cody was neck-deep in the drug operation and he had Olivia. Cody had driven by the barn earlier. He'd seen Jaden's patrol SUV. He would know that it was only a matter of time before he would be going down. He'd run. Was that what he'd been doing at the hardware store when Olivia showed up?

Had she seen something she shouldn't have? Caught him getting ready to skip town? What had he done to her?

Jaden thought of the broken jar on the floor, the drag marks in the jelly.

Cody had to have taken her. But where?

OLIVIA SAT UP and looked over at Cody. Her wrists were bound, but that wasn't all. He'd tied her bound wrists to the grab bar on the door so she couldn't jump out. Nor could she reach the steering wheel or attack him, both options she wished for right now as he slowed and made the turn down the road to Starling. Her stomach roiled as they rumbled along the road, the headlights giving her glimpses of the destruction ahead.

"What's going on, Cody?" she asked with a sigh as if bored by all this. Even as her heart raced, she told herself not to panic. She needed to keep all her senses sharp because she was going to get away from him. She had to.

"We're just going for a little ride," he said without looking at her.

"You were never a good liar."

His attention swung on her, his face contorting in anger. "Like you know anything about me. You left. You have no idea what I've had to do to keep from going stark raving mad." The venomous response alarmed her. "All I could think about was getting out of here, getting out from under that damn hardware store."

Her first instinct was to try to calm him down, to remind him that they were friends. "I'm sorry. I didn't know. I thought you didn't mind working with your dad."

Cory let out a bark of a laugh. "He had me over a barrel. Either I stayed and worked the store, or I walked away with nothing. Nothing. You think he would help me with college? With starting my own business? Not a chance. He started with nothing and made good, so he thought I should do the same." He seemed to grit his teeth. "He gave me no choice but to do what I did."

"No choice?" she asked almost in a whisper. He was driving slower now, but she could see what structures were still standing ahead getting closer against the skyline. As long as she could keep him talking...

The thought almost made her laugh out loud. No one knew where she was. No one was coming to save her. She was on her own. Her only chance to survive was to be ready. If he gave her an opening, she would take it to escape.

Cody looked over at her, and for a moment, he was the boy she'd grown up with. His gaze softened and the fury in his face dissolved. "I started my own drug business." She heard pride in his voice. "I made something out of myself."

Drugs? She tried not to show her revulsion as she listened to him talk about getting the supplies up on the Canadian border, hiring friends to bring them down and package them for distribution.

"It was a hell of an operation," he said proudly. "I should have done it sooner. Maybe you would have stayed."

She said nothing, gripping her hands together, her fingers white-knuckled. He'd never understood why she'd left to follow her dream. He'd just resented her for being able to do it. As it was, she'd learned that the grass wasn't greener. But it had made her figure out what she wanted. Montana, home and Jaden. And it had brought her back.

Cody looked lost in thought. She knew this wasn't about the two of them, no matter what he said. Nor about his father and the hardware store. This was about that night in Starling and Rob's murder. She didn't know how or why exactly, but she knew. "Who of the old gang work for you?"

He instantly perked up, anxious to talk about his enterprise. "Angie was my first hire. She'd rented this little barn outside of town to redo old furniture she found at garage sales." He scoffed. "I convinced her to use her skills and mine to make more money. She was like me. She wanted more. Her marrying Dean had been a mistake. He was still in love with Jenny. But as badly as she wanted to leave him, she couldn't until she had enough money to make it on her own. So I helped her."

They'd reached what was left of Starling. Even in the

glow of the headlights, what the tornado had left looked more menacing than it had in daylight.

Olivia shuddered as if she could feel the violence, the death, the disappointment that had happened here. It had left a pall over the place and seemed to invite more of the same.

"Emery?" Olivia asked, afraid of what would happen once he stopped driving, once he stopped talking.

"Emery? That lily-livered SOB?" He shook his head. "He was too chicken to go into business with me. He likes being a deadbeat."

The pickup slowed to a crawl. Cody brought it to a stop and cut the engine.

There was one name she hadn't mentioned, afraid that once she did, the ride was over. "What went wrong?" she asked as Cody fell silent. "Sounds like you had a viable business going."

He looked over at her in the darkness of the pickup's cab. This far away from town, she could see stars and just enough moon to throw a silvery haze over the landscape. It gave Starling a ghostly presence, making what she knew was coming all the more frightening.

"I gave Rob a job. He was making good money. But apparently it wasn't enough. He got greedy," he said somberly.

She knew but was afraid to say it.

He reached for the driver's-side door handle.

"You killed him."

Cody froze for a moment. He drew back his hand and turned again to look at her. "He thought I didn't know. It wasn't so much that I could have let it slide. He was my best earner. He took the most risk, driving up to the border with the furniture he helped Angie redo so we could hide the drugs inside."

He looked out into the darkness. She wondered if he was seeing this Starling or the one from Halloween night. "It was all too perfect, things were going too well." He shook his head. "As my old man often says, best not to make waves when you're all in the same boat."

"I don't understand," she said. "I left you down in the root cellar."

He smiled over at her. "It wasn't that deep that I couldn't get out using some of the shelving. I had to move quickly. I knew you'd be back soon, and I was going to need an alibi. I saw Rob. He'd survived the tornado, the bastard. He was going to get away with all of it, ripping me off and, worse, taking Angie with him. The fool woman had fallen for another loser."

"Rob and Angie?" she asked in surprise.

"They worked together every day in that old building she'd bought." His shrug said that there was no accounting for taste. "She was skimming money too. She just wasn't as greedy as Rob. They were running away together. Rob thought I didn't know."

"He was killed when a wall fell on him," she said, still trying to buy herself time.

"That was a stroke of luck—just like the tornado. I was counting on getting my chance that night before midnight. I knew Rob was planning to take off at midnight. Take off with a lot of my money. I'd planned to pick up something I could use as a weapon. As it was, I caught him next to that rock foundation wall. I got lucky."

"But you must have had to move quickly to get back into the root cellar before I came back with the rescue workers." She realized that she didn't have to encourage him to talk about it. He seemed to relish finally being able to tell someone how smart he was.

"I wasn't even sure that the wall killed him. But I didn't have time to stick around to find out. I had to get back before you returned. Anyone could have seen me, but no one did. I hurriedly scrambled back down into the hole, but as I did, some of the dirt caved in." He let out a laugh. "For a minute there, I thought I'd be buried alive. Got to see the irony in that, huh? Especially after we'd found those bones."

"But when I came back, you'd been injured."

He nodded, chuckling. "I heard you coming back. I decided to make it look good. The cave-in had uncovered a large rock stuck in the dirt wall of the root cellar. I reached up and managed to dislodge it, thinking that I would move away before it came down. Got my feet tangled up. That was the last thing I remembered until I woke up in the hospital."

"You didn't have amnesia, did you?"

"Nope, I remembered *everything*." There was a sharpness back in his voice. "That night, you had pretty much spelled out how you felt about me. I was never good enough for you."

"That's not true. You were my best friend."

"*Were* your best friend," he repeated and opened his door.

BACK OUT IN the alley, Jaden's mind raced. Cody was a loose cannon on the run, and he had Livie. Where would he take her? He could feel the clock ticking. He had to find her before it was too late. If it wasn't already too late.

The moment the first law-enforcement vehicle pulled up, Jaden rushed to it. He told the officer everything he knew, including that Cody Ryan had Olivia Brooks. Leaving the officer to secure and wait for a team to come in to process the scene, he got behind the wheel of his patrol SUV.

For a moment, he didn't know where to go or what to do. Like Olivia, Cody had been born and raised here. He knew the country. He would know where to go to get rid of Livie's body, and that place could be anywhere.

The realization came to him like a bolt of lightning out of the blue. The moment the thought surfaced, he knew where Cody had taken her.

Starling.

CODY CAME AROUND to Olivia's side of the pickup and opened the door. As long as her wrists were still bound and tied to the grab bar over her head, she couldn't try to get away. She reminded herself to wait until she had the advantage—if Cody ever gave her that.

He knew her, so he also knew how determined she could be. Backed in a corner, she would come out fighting. That meant he would also be waiting for her to try something.

"I don't understand why you're doing this," she said as he untied her from the grab bar and dragged her out into the darkness. "You got away with it. You fooled everyone!"

"Not everyone," he said under his breath. "Your boyfriend. He's coming for me."

"But what does that have to do with me?" she demanded.

"You're just collateral damage. You shouldn't have stopped by the hardware store tonight," he said with a shake of his head. "You caught me finishing up before I was skipping town. You and your damn crab apple jelly. I hate that crap and now it's all over the hallway at the shop. I couldn't leave you behind so you could tell the deputy what you'd over-heard in the alley."

"I didn't hear anything," she cried as he dragged her by her tied wrists up the hillside.

"But the spilled jelly," he said like a curse. "Jaden will

know you were there. He'll come looking for you. I can't take the chance that you'll tell him my plans."

"Cody, I swear I don't know your plans. I don't care about your plans. But if you kill me, Jaden will track you to the ends of the earth."

He stopped walking to turn on her. "It's like that between the two of you? But you weren't together."

"We had broken up, but I came home to see if he still felt the way I did," she said. After that kiss, she'd had hope. She'd been counting on Jaden finishing this investigation and then there wouldn't be any reason they couldn't find their way back together. At least, that had been her hope.

Cody seemed to think that Jaden knew about his drug business, that he would be coming after him. She could only wish. But Jaden wouldn't know Cody had her. He wouldn't know where Cody had taken her and now time was running out.

"Glad to hear this is going to break his deputy heart," Cody said, clearly taking satisfaction in that.

"You're going to kill me out of jealousy," she snapped, her anger overtaking her fear for a moment. She was furious with herself for thinking they could be friends and even more furious with him.

Cody smiled, the moonlight flashing on his teeth. "I wouldn't even venture a guess how many women have been murdered out of jealousy, but I bet it's a lot. No man wants to think he never mattered."

"You did matter. You still matter."

He laughed. "Not enough."

"Enough that I brought you jelly," she stressed.

"And signed your own death warrant." He jerked the binding on her wrists angrily as he continued to haul her up the hillside.

She could see the crime scene tape around the root-cellar hole ahead. It rustled in the breeze. Hadn't she known this was why he'd brought her here? Hadn't she known how it would end?

Unless she stopped him.

Chapter Eighteen

Jaden wanted to go after Livie lights and siren blaring. But he knew that would only warn Cody he was coming. *If* Cody had taken her to Starling, he reminded himself. The sooner he found out, the better. Better still if Cody didn't know he was coming for him until it was too late.

He tried not to second-guess himself as he tromped on the gas. There was little to no traffic on the road out of town. What he did encounter, he passed at high speed. Nothing would slow him down, given the urgency he felt to get to Livie.

The first time he'd seen her on the college campus his senior year, he'd fallen for her the moment he'd laid eyes on her. That moment in time was like a photo he'd snapped, a memory he could never forget. He'd never had that happen to him before. He'd known she was the woman he was going to marry.

He could find humor in that now since they hadn't married. Not yet, anyway, he mused as he drove. He'd lost hope for a while, but since that kiss… He smiled to himself, remembering that moment he knew.

She'd been coming out of one of the campus buildings with a couple of friends. Something one of them said had suddenly made her laugh. Just the sight of her had stopped him in his tracks, but it was the way she'd let herself laugh that had drawn him as if he'd lassoed and pulled her to him. She'd turned her face up to the sun, a joyous expression making her look radiant. Her long, silken blond hair seemed to float around her as she'd moved.

I'm going to marry that girl, he'd thought. But first he'd have to meet her, he'd amended, not in the least worried. It had felt meant to be. He still felt that way.

He looked at the highway through his headlights and couldn't bear the thought that something bad had already happened to her. He'd already called for backup to meet him at the abandoned community. It would take law enforcement from other towns too long to get there.

That meant he was on his own. All he could hope was that he got there soon enough. And that he wasn't wrong about where Cody had taken her. The backup hadn't been to help him anyway. It was so Cody didn't get away if things went south.

Jaden had no idea what to expect. Had it only been Cody who'd taken her? He hoped the man's friends wouldn't be involved. Either way, he had to assume that Cody would be armed. What worried him was why he'd take her back to Starling. Just to get rid of her body? Or was there something else Cody was planning to do out there?

The clock was ticking. He had no idea how long Cody had been gone from the hardware store with Livie. Nor did he know what the man had planned. Get rid of Livie's body and keep running?

Jaden just hoped there was time to get there, find him and stop him. He didn't want to think about what he would do if Cody hurt the woman he loved. He wouldn't need backup to take Cody to jail. If he let himself go, Cody would never see a cell. But then Jaden would never be in law enforcement again either. Right now, it seemed a fair trade-off.

He loved his career choice because he could find the bad guys and bring them to justice. Even as he reminded himself of that, he still feared what he would do when he got his hands on Cody Ryan.

It was his fear talking, he told himself.

With a curse, he shoved away the thought that he might be too late. She couldn't be gone. Wouldn't he feel that in his heart, if true?

CODY WAS THINKING about his future far from here as he worked his way through the debris toward what was left of the root cellar. It had been such an obvious place to get rid of Olivia's body. It felt meant to be. No one would look for her there because no one would know where she'd gone.

He liked the idea that some people—the deputy, for one—would think she'd run off with her high school boyfriend. Why not? It could have happened. If it wasn't for her being in love with the deputy. He cursed under his breath at the thought. Her loss. As his old man often said, there were a lot of fish in the sea.

Lost in dreams of how he'd spend all his money, he'd almost forgotten about Olivia.

Until she seemed to trip and stumble. He still had hold of her bound wrists, so, as she fell, it pulled him off balance—breaking his hold on her. As she hit the ground, he fell beside her.

Before he knew what was happening, she looped her bound arms around his throat and pulled, putting so much pressure on his windpipe that he couldn't breathe. She dug her heels in as she drove the rough rope of her bondage into his neck. He forced out a guttural sound as he clawed at the rope and fought for breath. It had happened so fast that she had him at a disadvantage, on the ground with her behind him. He couldn't breathe and the rope tore into his neck. If he didn't get her off of him soon, she was going to strangle him to death.

He quit trying to rip the rope from his throat. Stretching back, he clawed at her, trying to reach her face, her eyes. She managed to avoid his hands, but at least his attempts had forced her to let up on the pressure on his neck at little.

Getting a grip on one of her arms, he squeezed as hard as he could until she cried out. He wanted to call her names, but he didn't have enough air as he began to kick back at her legs while digging his fingers into the flesh of her arm.

He felt the pressure on him slacken, but then she reared as hard as she could, slamming his head back into hers. The blow stunned him, but only for a moment. He swung an elbow around and caught her in the side of the head.

With relief, he felt her body go limp. Swearing, he grabbed her arms, the pressure off his throat, and tossed them back over his head. Through blurred vision, he rose awkwardly from the ground. Maybe she'd hurt him, but she'd hurt herself as well, he saw through his fury. Her eyes were unfocused from the blow to the head and her nose was bleeding, maybe even broken.

He was breathing hard as he rubbed his bruised and scraped throat and looked down at her. He wanted to kick her, beat her into the ground, to take out all his anger and frustration on her. He pulled the gun from his pocket, telling himself to save his energy and just shoot her. Her eyes must have focused enough that she saw how close she was to dying right here on the hillside.

She closed her eyes, expecting a bullet. He tried to catch his breath, tried to keep to his original plan. Killing her here would mean he'd have to carry her dead body up the rest of the way to the root cellar. Yet it felt impossible to rein in his wrath. She symbolized everything he couldn't have.

But then she opened her eyes and looked at him with raw defiance. Her gaze said that he'd have to look in her eyes as he killed her. He pointed the gun at her head and told himself she wouldn't be that heavy to carry up the hill. Seconds passed, his finger on the trigger, her gaze locked with his.

With a curse, he swallowed back his rage, reminding himself that he didn't have a lot of time. He needed to take care of her, then get what he'd left up on this hillside and clear out.

"Get up." His voice sounded rough. He coughed and swore again. "Get up or so help me…"

She rose slowly, looking dizzy and a little disoriented. Two blows to the head had probably left her with a raging headache. That made him feel a little bit better.

"Move," he said, motioning with the gun. "Try something again and I'll empty every bullet in this gun into you."

Olivia looked as if all the fight had gone out of her. She finally saw him for who he was, not some boy she would wrap around her finger. Not some teenager she'd left pining for her. That Cody was gone, replaced by a dangerous man she didn't know.

JADEN TURNED OFF his headlights as he reached the road into Starling. It was hard to drive slowly, but he wasn't going far. He pulled over and cut the engine in a stand of trees that had weathered the storm. With luck, his vehicle wouldn't be seen or heard from Starling. He took his shotgun. He was already wearing his sidearm. Both were loaded. He climbed out, closing his SUV door quietly.

He could see Cody's pickup with hardware store logo on

the side parked up the road. Taking long strides, he headed for it, all the time watching the hillside for any movement.

A thin layer of clouds muted the moon and starlight, but he could see well enough when he reached Cody's pickup. Empty. No sign of a struggle that he could see. What he really hadn't wanted to see was blood—and he didn't.

The chilly breeze stung his face but he welcomed the cold. It kept him alert and sharp, he told himself. If Cody had heard his vehicle engine coming up the road, he might be lying in wait somewhere up there to ambush him.

He slowed and listened hard. Voices. He waited, hoping to catch Livie's. When he did, he felt his heart soar. She was still alive. All he had to do was get to her quickly. He could think of only one reason Cody had brought her here.

When they spoke again, he realized that they weren't far from the open root cellar. He needed to get closer. His options weren't good, given the mountains of debris spread across this hillside. There would be no charging up the hill. They would hear him coming as he bounded over what was left of the community, only to get himself and Livie killed.

He began to work his way through the debris that separated them until he could get a decent shot at Cody.

OLIVIA HURT ALL over from her struggle with Cody. She wiped at her nose with her sleeve as she walked. She could feel him behind her. Earlier, she'd thought for sure he'd kill her right there on the side of the mountain. He'd certainly wanted to. She'd seen it in his eyes.

She'd hoped that the Cody she'd known was still in there and that all she had to do was reach him. She'd thought she could talk him down and stop him from doing what she knew he had planned for her.

But she no longer did. She stumbled up the rest of the

hill, weaving her way through piles of splintered boards, piles of bricks and cement, portions of roofs and walls, to the spot where a small house had once stood.

Hadn't Jaden said his parents had lived there when he was a kid before they'd left Starling? It was gone now, leaving behind debris and a large dark hole in the ground that had once been a root cellar.

She feared she was about to suffer the same fate Evangeline had.

Feeling Cody directly behind her, Olivia moved slowly toward the open root-cellar chasm, knowing that once he got her down there it would be over. "This can't be the only reason we're here. Just to kill me?" she asked, surprised that she'd voiced her thoughts.

He shoved her forward. They were almost close enough that all he would have to do was give her a push and she'd tumble into the void.

She glanced down the hillside to where she'd heard Rob's body had been found and stopped abruptly. Cody jabbed her in the back with the barrel end of the gun. "Did you see that?"

"What?" He glanced down the hillside. But not long enough for her to take advantage of the misdirection, even if she felt strong enough to do so. The physical struggle with him had taken a lot out of her.

"I just saw someone," she said in a whisper. She pointed. "Down there. He went behind that house."

He looked at her, unsure, and she was afraid that she hadn't sold it well enough. "What are you trying to pull?" he demanded.

"I'm telling the truth. It was a man. He was…watching us." She opened her mouth and screamed "Help!" as loud as she could.

CODY GRABBED OLIVIA'S ARM, dragged her to him and clamped his hand down hard over her mouth. He told himself it was time to finish this. Shove her into the hole, kick some dirt down on her and take care of the reason he had planned all along to come here tonight long before she'd shown up at the wrong time at the hardware store.

What stopped him was that he wasn't so sure she was lying. What if she had seen a man? But why would someone come out here tonight? Maybe for the same main reason he had. That was what really changed his mind. He realized he might need a human shield. As badly as he wanted to pitch her into the open root cellar, he realized it might benefit him to keep her with him.

He'd been so certain that no one had known what he'd been hiding up here. But Rob had. With a silent curse, he recalled that he'd foolishly brought Krystal with him on one of his late-night trips to Starling. He'd ordered her to stay in the pickup while he'd trudged up the hillside with his full backpack. But Krystal never did what she was told. He hadn't thought much of it, though. He never thought she'd tell anyone, knowing what he'd do to her if she did.

But she must have told Rob. And who else?

Holding Olivia by the back waistband of her jeans, he pushed her in front of him to the corner of one of the still-standing old houses. Pulling Olivia close, he peered around the corner.

No one. Yet he couldn't shake the feeling that they weren't alone. He told himself it was the drugs. They made him paranoid and anxious. He closed his eyes, only to have a flash of memory from Halloween night. He'd climbed out of the root cellar to kill Rob and found him digging in the debris. He'd known at once what Rob had been looking for—and why Rob had agreed to come to Starling that night. He knew about his boss's stash.

Cody had wanted to kill him for skimming from him. But once he'd realized that Rob knew about the money stashed here on this hillside, he wasn't about to let the man take everything he'd work so hard for. He'd known then that it was time to kill him.

That night, he'd felt a kind of fury like none he'd ever known. It still amazed him that he hadn't attacked Rob right then and there, blowing his alibi and any chance he would have had to get back in the root cellar in time. But he'd kept his cool. Finding Rob digging under the rock foundation wall, he'd realized that the man hadn't known exactly where the loot was hidden.

Moving swiftly, the clock ticking, Cody had slipped around the foundation wall and pushed with a strength that still boggled his mind. The wall toppled, but not before Rob had seen it coming and tried to scramble out of the way.

But the man hadn't been fast enough. Cody had stared at the body crushed beneath the wall. Only Rob's head and arms had managed to get free. He'd seen the shine of the man's eyes. Rob had been trying to say something, possibly beg for his life, mumbled words bubbling out in blood. It would have been so easy to finish him, but Cody hadn't had the time. He'd had to get back to the root cellar.

Reliving that night now, though, only made him more edgy. If Rob had survived, he would have turned on him. Good thing he hadn't. Like tonight. He couldn't leave Olivia alive. It was that simple.

But first he had to get to where he'd hidden the bags of money. He assured himself that if they'd been found by search and rescue or the state crime investigators, he would have heard about it.

Still, if someone else was really out here tonight with them, the person could already have found his stash and could be carrying it off right now.

He pushed Olivia ahead of him, keeping a strong grip on her to keep her from escaping as they descended the hillside. In the moonlight, he made out the old stone pump house below them. It didn't surprise him that it was still standing. The rock walls were thick, the space inside tight.

As they got closer, he saw that the door stood open, making his heart rabbit in his chest. Of course, it would have been searched. But had they found anything?

Too dark to tell if his secret hiding place had been discovered, he forced Olivia inside. She cried out when her hip connected with the rusted old-fashioned hand pump. He held her against it with his body as he took out his phone and used the flashlight to shine it on the stone wall. Relief made him weak. The loose large rock and the hiding space behind it that he'd discovered as a boy hadn't been found.

Putting away his phone, he worked the stone out, dropping it to the wooden floor with a thud. Then he reached in, still worried the bags wouldn't be there. Rescue and searchers had been all over Starling, not to mention law enforcement. Hurriedly, he reached deeper into the space between the stones, his panic growing until his hand brushed the canvas of a bag.

He let out a laugh as he began to pull out one bag after another. He still couldn't believe his luck. For a while tonight, things hadn't been going well. Olivia showing up at the hardware store had thrown him. But now he felt a lightness that reassured him it was all going to turn out just fine.

Or it would—once he took care of Olivia.

She hadn't seen anyone out here with them. She had just

been trying to throw him off. It had worked, but soon her time would be up.

"Is this why you killed Rob?" she asked as he opened one of the bags, half-afraid he'd been wrong and the bag would be filled with paper instead of hundred-dollar bills. With a laugh, he confirmed it was full of money. His money.

"There were a lot of reasons Rob had to go," Cody said, his relief warming him to the subject. Confession, it turned out, did feel good, especially when it didn't cost him anything. "I just got lucky Halloween night. I knew that if he got arrested, he'd take me down with him."

"Wasn't he leaving town for a job in Seattle?" she asked, sounding as if in pain with the old pump handle digging into her leg and hip.

"That bull about some great job out on the coast, buying a condo." Cody shook his head with disgust. "Who did Rob think he was kidding? It was no secret that he wanted out of the business. He was scared of getting caught. Emery treated Rob like he was some kind of hero, always saying that Rob had saved his life. What a joke, those two."

He froze to listen as he felt the hair quill on the back of his neck. He'd heard something. A footfall on loose rocks? The clang of twisted metal?

Olivia had been lying about seeing someone, hadn't she?

Chapter Nineteen

Jaden had cut across the lower part of the hillside, working his way through the debris, seeking cover where he could find it. He finally reached a spot where he could start up the hillside. They were standing next to the root-cellar hole. He feared that Cody would throw her down before he could get a shot at him and started to move toward them when he realized that he'd been seen.

In the moonlight, he could see them both looking in his direction. He froze, back pressed to the shadowed darkness of what was left of one of the houses. He cursed his luck. There was no way he could get a clear shot from this distance. On top of that, now Cody would be looking for him.

To his surprise, Cody seemed to change his mind. He pushed Livie ahead of him as they started down the hillside. Cody was keeping her where he could use her as a shield. Bastard. All Jaden could do was wait and hope for a shot. But that was going to be difficult since Cody had taken a path on the other side of the debris. Jaden was only getting glimpses of them.

Where was he taking her? To his surprise, they appeared headed for a small stone structure that was still standing farther down the hill. Jaden wanted to get closer but there was too much rubble. He watched as Cody and Livie disappeared into the tiny building.

He considered trying to get down there but realized that he stood a better chance once they emerged. He had no doubt that Cody would take Livie back up the hill as a shield until he felt he didn't need her anymore.

But why the little stone building? Because there was something he wanted to retrieve? Of course, he would have needed a place to hide his ill-gained money. Cody knew this place. But once he collected it, then what? Jaden waited, growing more anxious. What if he was wrong? He'd been so sure that if Cody planned to kill her, he wouldn't want her body to be found. Why else would he bring her here?

The waiting was killing him. He couldn't understand what was taking so long. What if he was wrong and Cody killed her inside that small building? There was probably a well in there. He could dispose of her body down the well if it was large enough, deep enough.

He couldn't take it any longer, even knowing that if he'd been wrong, then Livie was already dead. He started to step away from the side of the house, but as he did, the boards under him gave way and he dropped into darkness, coming down hard.

Cody froze. He'd heard what Olivia had. She felt the change in him. He was scared. But so was she. What she'd heard sounded like boards breaking and then a duller crash followed by silence.

It was the silence that terrified her. Cody must have heard the same thing. But had it been someone out there? Or an animal? She'd been pretending she'd seen someone earlier, trying to buy time. As paranoid as Cody was acting, she was thankful it had helped. Otherwise, she would already be in that root cellar, probably under enough dirt that she would no longer be breathing.

The thought that it really might be someone gave her hope. If it was just her and Cody alone out here tonight, Olivia wasn't sure how she would survive. As jumpy as he was, he would be watching her closely. And he had a loaded gun. She felt as if he had reached a point where he had nothing to lose. Even if by chance someone tried to stop him, it would probably only get them killed. He was intent on getting rid of her and leaving.

That the law would eventually catch up to him didn't help. By then, she would have been dead for weeks, months or even years.

"Take these and don't drop them," Cody ordered as he shoved two of the bags at Olivia. "We're going to head back up the hill. I'll be right behind you with a gun at your back."

The bags of money were heavy as she stepped out of the pump room into the night. What was left of Starling appeared eerie in the thin light of the partial moon. She shivered against the cold breeze as she looked for movement. If someone was out there, she didn't see them. Because they'd fallen and either hurt or killed themselves.

Earlier in the day, her mother had predicted a snowstorm. Sharon hadn't been wrong. It had snowed in the mountains while she and her mother were making the jelly.

Yet there was no doubt that the temperature had dropped here in the valley. She could hear Cody behind her, almost feel his desperation. Several times, she glanced back to catch him looking around as if still not sure there wasn't someone out there in the shadows of the Starling skeletons.

Fortunately, he'd had to pocket the handgun he'd pulled earlier to carry the heavy canvas bags he'd retrieved. He seemed to be working himself up into a state as if afraid he'd come this far to lose everything.

Olivia knew the feeling. She'd come home to make amends for her bad decisions. She'd ended up alienating the two men she'd cared about. Was that why she hadn't noticed how much Cody had changed? He'd been angry on Halloween, but his whole demeanor had changed when she'd suggested they go back to the vehicles and leave.

Now she understood why. He'd planned to kill Rob Perkins that night. What he hadn't planned for was the tornado, but even that he'd used to his advantage.

That the boy next door had grown up to be a killer shocked her. She'd loved that young Cody. She could understand the pressure he was under with his father and the hardware store. He'd worked in that store from the time he was a boy, only to realize that he was trapped. He could have walked away, but without money and nowhere to go, he'd stayed and started his own lucrative but deadly business that would eventually get him killed.

It all seemed such a waste as she worked her way through the debris in the moon and starlight. Everywhere there were hazards. Splintered boards, broken glass, pieces of twisted, sharp metal. Something caught on her jeans. She heard it rip as she tried to pull free and felt whatever it was bite into her skin.

Her head still hurt from earlier, the dizziness making walking hard without worrying about what might attack her legs. The blows had weakened her. She didn't think she could get the better of Cody again—let alone fight him off.

JADEN HAD DROPPED a half dozen feet, landing hard and pulling broken boards down on him as he fell to his knees. As he'd tried to catch himself, he'd felt nails ripping through his flesh. Blood began to run down his arms as he fought to get to his feet in the broken boards around him. The moment he did, he knew his ankle was badly sprained. He could barely put weight on it.

Pulling out his flashlight, he shone it around. He'd fallen into a space with a dirt floor. He had no idea how large it was or if there was a way out. He looked up, afraid he might not be able to climb out and what that would mean for Livie.

Pushing aside the panic, he knelt to run his flashlight beam under the boards that had collapsed with his weight. If it was a basement, there had to be a way out. Dropping into an awkward crawl, his ankle aching in pain, he moved under the collapsed building until he found what he was looking for.

Ahead, he saw crumbling concrete stairs, but they, too, were blocked by debris. The feel of a breeze on his face gave him hope that there was an opening, and he was going to be able to get out. He moved some boards and other wreckage. Then he shone his flashlight into the darkness. It lit an opening a few steps above him. He began to climb, his only thought getting to Livie.

OLIVIA SLOWED AS ahead she saw the gaping black hole of the root cellar. Soon it would be over, she told herself. She rebelled at the thought, even as her mind raced for a way to save herself.

"Cody," she said, turning to look back at him. Out of the corner of her eye, she saw Jaden. He'd come out of a pile of rubble below them on the hillside. Her heart leaped, then fell. He was still too far away to help with a lot of tornado debris between them. She had to stall. Her life depended on it. Jaden was there. He was coming for her. "You don't want to do this."

In answer, he shoved her forward. *Stall*, she told herself. *Do whatever you have to do, but don't let him kill you. Jaden is trying to get to you.* She took a slow, tentative step and then another. Jaden had found her. She didn't know how, but she loved him for it. Ahead, the hole loomed black in the moonlight. A couple more steps and she would be down there in the dark.

"Stop right there," Cody said from behind her. "Drop the bags."

Olivia felt that spark of resistance that ran deep in her. With all her strength, she took another step and heaved both bags toward the open pit of the root cellar.

JADEN HAD LOST crucial time. He had dragged himself out. When he could finally stand, he realized how badly he was hurt. He wasn't sure how far he could walk on his ankle. It wasn't broken; at least, he hoped not. As badly as it hurt to put any weight on it, he ignored the pain and headed up the hillside. To keep from being seen, Jaden had previously been forced to stay on a winding path of tornado wreckage.

Now, though, he had no choice but to leave behind any cover and charge up the hillside as best he could with his ankle wanting to give out. He could see that Cody and Livie were almost to the dark abyss of the root cellar. If Cody saw him, Jaden had no doubt that the man would use Livie as a shield and start firing. All Jaden could hope was that Cody wasn't much of a marksman.

That was when he saw Livie turn and look in his direction. Earlier, he'd thought they'd both seen him. But this time, it was just Livie. There was no doubt that she saw him.

Cody shoved her toward the open pit. Jaden tried to run up the hill, but his ankle turned and he fell, crashing into more debris. He ground his teeth, the pain so intense he thought he would black out. The moment it passed, he was on his feet again.

Up on the hill, he saw Livie throw the large bags she'd been carrying into the old root cellar. There was no doubt that she would be next. Bleeding and limping, his leg apparently hurt worse than he'd thought, he kept moving toward them. He had to get to Livie before it was too late.

"No!" CODY LET out a howl of anger and misery as he watched the bags filled with his money fly through the air over the opening—and then plummet. "You stubborn, impossible woman!"

Dropping the two bags he had carried up from the stone well house, he lunged forward to strike her in the back with his fist. His momentum shoved her forward. As his money hit the bottom of the root cellar's dirt floor, Olivia followed them down.

Propelled forward, Cody stumbled behind her, stopping so close to the unstable edge of the chasm that he almost went in after her. He teetered there, his anger feeling as if it were eating him up inside. If he could have gotten his hands on her neck, he would have choked the life out of her. What had ever made him think he could love this woman? Didn't he recall how stubborn she'd been as a kid? As a girlfriend? He'd told himself he liked a strong woman. Ha! he thought now.

For a moment, she didn't move. He stood waiting to see if she took a breath. Time seemed suspended. He breathed heavily, the exertion of his anger making his chest hurt. He really could use a little something to steady himself. Once he got to the pickup, he'd dig into his supply.

Not now, though. He just had to be sure that Olivia wouldn't be getting out of that hole alive. She still hadn't moved. Maybe she'd hit her head. Maybe she was already dead.

Not that it mattered at this point. If she hadn't tossed his money down there, he had planned to cave in the side of the hole and bury her alive, if that was what it took. Then all he would have had to do was get out of Starling, get on the road, disappear before the law came after him. He'd known it was just a matter of time the moment he'd seen Jaden at Angie's barn. He'd known then that it was time to leave for good.

Earlier, it had seemed so simple. Just tie up some loose ends, starting at the hardware store. He'd made the calls to some of his associates. He couldn't just leave without letting his father know how he felt about him. It had taken four of them and a dolly to remove the old floor safe where his father kept his "retirement" money.

While they were at it, they'd loaded up everything they could haul of any value. If Olivia hadn't shown up when she had, they would have taken even more.

Now he just had to deal with this problem. He stared down at her and his bags of money and swore. "I can see that you're breathing," he said through gritted teeth. "Stand up."

She made no move to do so.

"I need you to stand up. You don't want me to come down there."

She let out a laugh and rolled to her side. "Come on down," she yelled as if she wanted the whole world to hear. She sounded as if the fall had knocked the breath out of her. But when she smiled up at him, he realized that the bags of money had broken her fall.

He cursed. He was pretty sure he could get back out of the old root-cellar hole, even though the rescue crew had broken a lot of the shelving in their attempt to get him out

Halloween night. "Trust me, you don't want me to come down there," he said, raising his voice as well. He'd convinced himself that they were alone on the hillside. It didn't matter if she wanted to scream her head off.

"Oh, why not, Cody?" she shouted. "Afraid I might hurt you?"

He kicked dirt down on her, some of it hitting her in the face. That shut her up for the moment. She seemed to have forgotten that he was still in control. She sat up, wiping away the dirt and spitting a couple of times. He'd taught her how to spit like a boy one day in their tree house. She looked up at him again, defiance in her dirty face. "I'm waiting! Jump on down here!"

"Olivia, damn it, I never wanted it to end like this," he said, trying to sound as conciliatory as possible, yet still yelling too. "I would have let you be if you hadn't shown up at the store when you did."

"You mean when you were stealing your father blind?"

He doubled up his fists. "Just throw the bags up to me. I won't kill you. I'll just leave. Maybe you can even figure out a way to climb out. Or someone will find you. I could call anonymously once I'm down the road and tell your deputy where he can find you."

She laughed and shook her head. "Do you really expect me to believe that? What happened to you, Cody? You want everyone to feel sorry for you because you felt your father did you wrong. How about you stop making excuses for the decisions you've made? You broke the law. Now you're going to have to pay for it. Killing me isn't going to help. I don't think you're going to be able to live with the guilt." He gave her a smirk and kicked more dirt into the hole. This time she covered her face.

When she glanced up, he could see her eyes. They seemed

lit by the moonlight. He tried not to shudder at the look in those eyes, let alone her words. "I will come back and haunt you, Cody. I promise you. You'll never find peace for what you're about to do."

He took a step back. "Great speech, Olivia. Unfortunately, you're assuming I have a conscience." His laugh didn't ring true, even for him. "I don't. So come to me in my dreams all you want. You don't scare me." He pulled the gun from his pocket. "But if you don't throw those bags up to me right now," he raged, "I'm going to start shooting you—not kill you, just wound you so you can lie there bleeding to death, and no one will be able to save you."

"You don't think I know I'm dead no matter what? I just hope I don't bleed all over your money, Cody," she shouted as she pulled the closest bag to her chest, her look daring him to pull the trigger.

He took the dare.

Chapter Twenty

The loud argument between the two covered the sound of Jaden's footfalls as he scrambled up the hill as fast as he could, hurling himself forward with all his strength. His body took the stabs of splintered wood, glass shards and torn jagged metal as if no longer able to feel pain. He knew he was doing more damage, had already done damage to himself, but he couldn't let it stop him.

He was almost to Cody when he heard the report. The shot echoed across the hillside into the night. Breathing hard, weapon in his hand, he started to fire but was almost on the man. More than anything, he was afraid Cody would get off another shot at Livie trapped in the hole below him.

Jaden didn't stop. He launched himself. Cody, caught completely off guard, went down hard, Jaden landing on top of him. He started to grab for Cody's gun but realized it was no longer in the man's hand. He took a quick look for it around them. Those few seconds gave Cody a chance to catch his breath. Jaden took an elbow to his head that momentarily dazed him as Cody began to fight back as if his life depended on it.

He put an arm against the man's neck as he struggled to roll Cody to his stomach so he could handcuff him. "Livie!" he cried. "Livie?"

"I'm all right," she called back.

His heart soared at the sound of her voice as Cody kicked wildly, bucking and swinging his arms. A part of him wanted Cody to put up a fight, even relished the idea. But Cody was strong and desperate, and Jaden was becoming more aware of his injuries. It would be a fight to the finish of one of them. Jaden realized he had no choice as Cody fought wildly to throw him off—toward the black hole next to them.

Whatever drug the man was on, it had made him stronger. They were too close to the hole. Jaden tried to roll Cody away from it, fearing they would cave the dirt onto Livie. She was still alive. He hung on to that as he used everything he'd been taught in combat to restrain the man.

But Cody was a dirty fighter. That, added to his strength and desperation and Jaden's body's weakness, had the deputy feeling himself losing the battle.

OLIVIA HAD HEARD the gun drop down into the hole. It was too dark to see exactly where it had landed, but she was sure that was the sound she'd heard. She began to feel around for it, thankful that Cody had only fired a warning shot into the dirt inches from her head earlier. She'd been right about him not wanting to get blood on his money. Or maybe he hadn't wanted to kill her yet because it would mean he'd have to climb into the hole and dig his bags of money out from under her dead body.

She couldn't believe he'd still held out hope that he could talk her into throwing the bags up to him. The drugs he'd been taking must have addled his brain. Moving her hands palm-down across the dirt, she hunted as hurriedly as possible to find the gun. She could hear the struggle up on the ledge. Dirt came falling down, making her all the more frantic to find the gun before the wall of dirt caved in on her.

Her hand touched something cold as steel. She grabbed the gun, just as another chunk of the dirt wall collapsed. She barely had time to throw herself out of the way before it covered one of her legs. She quickly dug herself out, desperate to stop the fight that was about to bury her alive.

Gun tucked into her waistband, she hurried and grabbed the heavy bags of money, piling them on top of the dirt that had caved into the pit. Then she began to climb quickly upward, afraid the moving earth would cave in. She saw at once that she wouldn't be able to get out without help. But she could get high enough.

In the faint moonlight, she could see that Jaden had Cody down and was reaching for his handcuffs. Cody grabbed a handful of dirt and threw it into Jaden's eyes, then pushed him off and was going for Jaden's gun.

She could see that Jaden was hurt, his clothing torn and bloodstained. That sound she'd heard that had made her think someone had fallen through boards, she knew now it had to have been Jaden.

Olivia aimed the gun at Cody, trying not to see the boy she'd grown up with, her best friend, her high school sweetheart. He had wrenched the deputy's weapon, had it in his hand, started to point it at Jaden's head.

She pulled the trigger.

JADEN COULDN'T SEE, his eyes full of dirt. He'd been fighting Cody blindly when he'd felt his weapon being pulled from his holster. He lunged at where he thought the man was, heard the gunshot, felt the splatter of blood hit his face and thought he'd been hit. He wiped frantically at his eyes, expecting another shot and then another. All he could think about was Livie.

If he died here, she would too.

He heard her calling his name as his vision finally cleared enough to find Cody lying next to him. For a moment, he thought the man had taken his weapon to shoot himself. Then he looked up and saw Livie. She still held Cody's gun in her hand, resting it on the edge of the hole. She was crying as he crawled forward, stopping short of the edge to take the gun and hold her hand.

"Cody?" she whispered.

He shook his head as a wail of sirens filled the air. "Let's get you out of there."

Chapter Twenty-One

The rest of the night was a blur of sirens and lights. Jaden had managed to get Livie out of the root cellar by using all four of the canvas bags of money. She had climbed out into his arms as more of the unstable earth tumbled down into the hole.

With the arrival of help, EMTs saw to both his and Livie's injuries. He vaguely remembered them encouraging him to go to the hospital, but he was more worried about Livie and what she'd been through. Nor had he wanted to let her get out of his sight. The whole ordeal had left him afraid that he still might lose her.

There was so much he wanted to say to her. He worried that after everything she'd been through, the last place she'd want to be was in Montana—with him.

A state trooper arrived and took photographs and statements from them. When the coroner showed up to transport Cody's body to the morgue, he saw Jaden's injuries bandaged up temporarily by the EMTs and said, "Someone get this man to the hospital right now."

That was the last he remembered until he woke up in the hospital to find a doctor standing over him. "How are you feeling?"

He hurt all over, but he was alive. "Livie?" The doctor frowned. "Olivia Brooks?"

"Patched up and released."

"I have to see her," Jaden said and tried to sit up.

The doctor put a hand to his shoulder. "She's just fine. You, on the other hand, aren't going anywhere. You lost a lot of blood. We had to operate on your leg. Those were some nasty wounds. You're also not going anywhere on that other leg of yours."

He looked down to see a cast on his ankle. "Broken?"

The doctor shook his head. "Badly sprained. It's going to take some time for those tendons to heal. So just relax if you want to be able to walk again. You're going to be here for a while so we can make sure there isn't any infection."

He glanced around. No landline. "Can I at least get a phone to make a call?"

There was a twinkle in the doctor's eye. "To call Livie? Not necessary. She's right outside and very anxious to see you."

Jaden let out the breath he'd been holding and relaxed back on the bed.

"I'll tell her you're awake after your surgery. Remember what I said about taking it easy, Deputy." He smiled and left.

A moment later, Livie came in. She moved quickly to his bed and took his free hand. He hadn't even noticed how hooked up he was to machines. Had he looked, he could have seen his heart rate take off at the sight of her.

"I was so scared when I learned how injured you were." Tears filled her eyes. "All the time you were busy saving me… You had to be in so much pain."

He smiled. "I don't remember. All I could think about was getting to you and making sure you were safe."

She squeezed his hand. "Thanks to you, I am."

"Livie." His voice filled with emotion. "I was so afraid that I'd lost you. I've been such a fool—"

She touched her finger to his lips and shook her head. "You were right. I didn't know what I wanted. For years, I had this plan. Then you came along, and I didn't see how I could have both. I felt I had to stick to my plan."

He kissed her finger and took her hand. "I never wanted to keep you from it."

"I know. I thought a clean break was the best thing so neither of us got derailed on our plans."

He chuckled at that. "I was already derailed. I realized I didn't want to continue on to law school. When I got the opportunity to go to the academy, I took it. After we broke up and you left, I was lost without you. But becoming a deputy…" He grinned. "I think I found my calling."

She laughed. "I'd say so." She leaned down to give him a kiss.

He swallowed, his throat having gone dry. "What are your plans now?"

"If you're asking if I'm taking off again…" She shook her head. "I'm staying. You're going to need someone to look after you when you get out of here. That's if you—"

"Only if you'll marry me. You do have some idea of what it might be like being the wife of a deputy sheriff. Do you still want to?"

Livie nodded, her eyes filling with tears. She reached into her pocket and pulled out the engagement ring he'd given her not all that long ago.

He took it from her and met her gaze. "Remember the last time I asked you to marry me?"

"It was beautiful, but that was then. This is now. After everything we've been through, nothing can be more special than this moment."

He shook his head. "You're amazing. I want to spend the rest of my life with you, Olivia Brooks. Will you be my wife, my partner, my lover, my best friend?"

"I will," she said, her voice breaking as he slipped the ring onto her finger. Laughing and crying, she bent to kiss him.

He laughed but quickly grew serious again. "You *are* amazing. I mean that. You saved my life."

"And you saved mine. We make a pretty good team, don't you think?"

"I do, but let's not do anything like this again, okay?" he said as he drew her closer. "I promise that living in Fortune Creek, things will be much quieter and a whole lot less dangerous."

She laughed. "I guess we'll see about that."

Chapter Twenty-Two

For weeks, Olivia had stayed close to the rehab center after Jaden had been released from the hospital. They'd spent hours getting to know each other again—and silently coming to terms with what had happened that last night in Starling.

It was something they didn't talk about, but she suspected he was as haunted by it as she was. She'd killed Cody, her once neighbor, friend and high school sweetheart. He'd turned into a man she hadn't recognized. A killer. A drug dealer. A drug user. A man who was willing to kill again to save himself from capture.

When she'd told her mother about that night, Sharon Brooks had been shocked. "Do you realize what would have happened if not for your quick thinking?" she demanded. Tears had filled her eyes an instant before she'd grabbed her daughter and tugged her into a hug. "I've always thought I wasn't much of a mother to you. Better than my own, but that's not saying much." She'd pulled back to look at Olivia as if seeing her for the first time. "I must have done something right to have such an amazing daughter."

Now, as Olivia finished packing, she was glad she hadn't kept anything from her apartment. When she'd quit her job and moved out of her furnished apartment, she'd realized that she hadn't collected anything. Not even memories she'd wanted to pack.

"Is that it?" her mother asked, glancing around her daughter's old bedroom. It looked exactly like it had when Olivia had gone away to college all those year ago.

"You'll come up a few days before the wedding, right?" Her mother nodded. "Jaden has you a room at the hotel there."

"Where the wedding's going to be."

"Yes." She felt like she should say more. "Thank you for everything."

"I didn't do anything," her mother said with a shrug.

"You did." She stepped to her and hugged her, realizing how thin her mother seemed. "You'll come for dinner so I can fatten you up." Sharon huffed but Olivia could tell she liked the idea. "I'll come down to visit when I can, but you'll always be welcome. Did I tell you that Jaden and I are planning to start a family right away?" She saw her mother's eyes light up. "Well, I'd better get going."

Picking up her suitcase, she headed for the door.

"I've got something cooking on the stove, so I won't see you out."

Her mother had never liked goodbyes. "Then I'll see you before the wedding." She opened the door, glanced over her shoulder to see her mother in the kitchen, wiping her eyes. "Don't forget to bring some of your crab apple jelly," she called back and left.

Olivia felt teary-eyed herself as she walked away from the home where she'd been raised. But it wasn't goodbye. It was a new beginning. She would bring her children here. Her mother would teach them to cook and fuss over them.

She put her suitcase in the back of the car and climbed in behind the wheel. But she hadn't gotten very far down the road when she saw a rig coming toward her that she recognized. The vehicle slowed, an arm coming out the window to flag her over.

Slowing, she put down her window and pulled alongside in the middle of the road. This was rural Montana; there was no traffic. "Hi, Dean." She'd wondered how he was doing after all of this. He'd lost his wife, still hadn't completely recovered from the injuries he'd sustained during the tornado and seemed a sad figure with so many of his friends gone. "You all right?" she asked when he said nothing.

"I heard you were leaving for Fortune Creek. The deputy already up there?"

She nodded. "I'm on my way now. Something wrong?"

"I just wanted to offer best wishes on your engagement."

"Thank you, but won't I see you at the wedding?" she asked.

"I'll have to get back to you on that." He looked down the highway. Still no traffic. "Well, I should get going. You take care of yourself."

"You too." He drove off. She watched him go in her side mirror for a moment before putting up her window and continuing along the road toward the turnoff to Fortune Creek.

It wasn't until she'd made the turn and was headed north on the way to her new home, her new life and her soon-to-be husband that a thought nudged her.

Where had Dean been heading before he'd seen her? This road didn't really go anywhere except the mountains. Unless he'd been using it as a shortcut to his wife's barn. Wasn't that property off-limits until after the trial?

Chapter Twenty-Three

Olivia had never been to Fortune Creek. Jaden had told her it was small, but *tiny* might have been closer to the truth. The town was in the northwest corner of the state, a rock's throw from the Canadian border. That whole part of the state was lawless except for the small sheriff's office where her husband-to-be worked.

She saw at once that the town was wild country, set in the mountains surrounded by pines, lots of pines, and rocky cliffs. The closest place of any size was Eureka, miles away, across the narrow Lake Koocanusa that crossed the border into Canada. It made the small Montana town she'd grown up in seem metropolitan.

Jaden, once healed enough to return home, had gone on ahead. She'd taken a few days to pack and spend time with her mother before hitting the road. The first thing she saw when she drove into town was the historic Fortune Creek Hotel with its wide porch across the front.

She'd done a little research on the place she would soon be living in. The all-wood structure had been built in the 1930s by a wealthy Easterner who'd wanted a hunting lodge for his many friends. Since then, it had changed little structurally. A tall, rather skinny building, it rose to four floors with only four large rooms per floor.

The rest of the town was a series of small, narrow buildings. There was a convenience store/gas station, a café and a few empty buildings. But what caught her eye was a boutique with a bright display in the front window. Jaden had told her that the sheriff's wife, Molly, had opened it. She collected unique things from all over the world to sell there.

It was definitely somewhere Olivia planned to explore, but first she wanted to see her fiancé. She drove only a little farther to find the town ended at a stream. Turning around, she drove back to the sheriff's office.

Like the rest of the town, it also was small and narrow, with an apartment upstairs where she and Jaden would be living until the wedding. Getting out, she breathed in the mountain air ripe with pine scent. Jaden had already warned her about Helen Graves, the sixtysomething dispatcher.

As she pushed open the door, she spotted the gray-haired Helen behind a desk, knitting something large with variegated yarn. "Hello," she said as she let the door close behind her.

The woman looked up, eyes squinting. "So, you're the fiancée, huh?"

"That would be me," she said with a nod.

Helen looked her up and down for a moment before she smiled. "You'll do. He's in the office with the sheriff. You can go in." With that, she went back to her knitting.

Jaden was sitting in the small sheriff's office. He rose when he saw her and introduced her to his boss, Sheriff Brandt Parker. They exchanged a few niceties. Then Jaden suggested he help her unload her car and see the apartment upstairs.

"So, what do you think?" he asked, looking anxious as he waved an arm toward Fortune Creek.

"I think it's charming."

He grinned and pulled her to him for a kiss right there on the town's main street. Then he led her upstairs to the apartment. He still had a limp from his injuries at Starling, but the doctor had said he was healing nicely.

Later, Olivia wouldn't remember much about the small apartment over the sheriff's office. The moment the door had closed, she was in his arms and he was kissing her, and she'd felt as if she'd finally found her way home.

They hadn't been together like this since they'd broken off their engagement a year ago. Desire spiked through her, a wildfire of emotions. Her body tingled with expectation as he began to slowly unbutton her blouse, his gaze locked with hers. Her blouse dropped to the floor. He gave her an appreciative look as he took in her black lace bra, passion burning in his eyes.

She could feel her hard nipples straining against the lace as he dipped his head to take one aching tip in his mouth and then the other. Her bra dropped to the floor as she opened his shirt, pressing her palms against his muscled chest and then her breasts to the warmth and strength of him.

Jaden let out a groan of pleasure and the next moment they were tearing off the rest of their clothing. Laughing, they stumbled back to fall on the bed. Naked bodies melting together, they made love without restraint—at least, the first time.

It was late by the time they got around to unloading her car and walked down to the café for dinner. Jaden introduced her to everyone they came across. She felt her face flush with appreciation as the town seemed to welcome her with open arms.

Everyone wanted to know about the upcoming wedding

and seemed delighted to hear it would be in Fortune Creek at the hotel—and they were all invited.

Olivia felt a glow of warmth like none she'd ever known. She was excited and full of joy, so much so that she completely forgot about mentioning to Jaden that she'd seen Dean.

JADEN FELT AS if he were dreaming as he and Olivia walked back to the apartment after dinner. He hadn't let himself believe this was possible in the time the two of them were apart. But now here they were, together, engaged and planning their life in Fortune Creek.

He stopped to point out the full moon lolling over the top of the pines and pulled Livie close. "Do you think you could be happy here?"

She nodded and smiled up at him. "I'd be happy anywhere with you, but I'm already falling in love with this town. The people are so friendly. Even Helen, kind of."

He laughed at that as they continued down the street. It wasn't until later that night, the two of them lying in bed together, that they talked about Starling and the case. He was still working to tie up the loose ends, but basically, it was over.

Angie had been picked up in Washington and was being brought back to stand trial. Rob and Cody were dead. The town was still grieving. Emery had closed up his shop, getting on one of his motorcycles, Krystal on the back, and taking a trip down to California. Both were required to come back for the trial.

During the weeks Jaden and Livie had been healing from the ordeal they'd barely lived through, they hadn't talked about it. Instead, they had talked about the future. There was the upcoming wedding, the move to Fortune Creek and where they would live.

Olivia said she was looking forward to being a wife. They'd both agreed that they wanted to start a family, buy a house and put down roots.

Now, though, in the darkness of their small apartment over the sheriff's office, they talked about the case and their near-death experiences.

"It's a miracle I lived through the tornado," Livie said.

"Cody saved your life that night."

She nodded. "Only because he needed an alibi."

"I think there was more to it than that. He loved you. How could he not?"

"We both loved each other growing up, but that boy I knew was gone. Some of it was the drugs, but a lot of it was his bitterness. He'd never really been trapped at the hardware store. He'd used that as an excuse. Such a waste."

Jaden agreed. "He was looking for an easy way out, though I don't think he would have ever left town if he hadn't been forced to run. For a lot of people, leaving the safety and security of what you know is just too hard." He looked over at Livie. "But not for you. That's another reason Cody resented you. You were a lot braver than him, and he knew it."

"I'm not sure how brave I was. But I was determined— to a fault."

"Well, now you have your business degree."

"Molly was impressed," she said with a laugh. "She seems excited for me to be working with her since she spends so much time on the road looking for more product for the store. I like her."

"I thought you would." He pulled her close. "We're going to be okay here, aren't we?"

She nodded. "About that night when you found me in Starling. I can't believe as injured as you were…" Her voice broke.

"At one point I thought I was going to have to crawl up that hill," he said. "But nothing could keep me from getting to you." He kissed her. "I love you, Livie. Always have. Is your mother going to be all right with you marrying me?"

She laughed, brushing at tears. "She's excited that I'm closer to home. And, of course, she's excited about the wedding. She never had one of her own. She can be…prickly, but she'll grow on you, I promise." He chuckled. "She really is excited about us giving her grandbabies."

"Me, too," he whispered. "Maybe we should work on that right now? What do you think?" She answered with a kiss.

IT AMAZED OLIVIA what a small town the whole state of Montana felt like. She and Jaden had posted their wedding announcement in the local shopper. It was what was done in small-town Montana since everyone in the community was invited.

On Thanksgiving, her mother had come up for the local feast down at the café. Alice, the café owner, put it on every year. Olivia couldn't believe how warm and welcoming everyone was. It was clear that they all loved Jaden and were happy for the two of them.

Ash Hamilton, over at the hotel, had told them not to worry. He had plenty of room. Local café owner Alice Weatherbee was to cater the affair and promised there would be plenty of food. The local bar would be furnishing the booze.

"Are you sure about an open bar?" Olivia had asked.

"Don't worry. Anyone who drinks too much will be put up at the hotel," Jaden had assured her.

Sharon Brooks had arrived two days early for the wedding to help. "This place is really nice," her mother had said of the hotel room Jaden had gotten for her. She'd sounded surprised. "The town, though, seems a little...small."

Olivia had laughed, surprised she wasn't more nervous as the wedding loomed. She couldn't wait to become Mrs. Olivia Montgomery. She and Jaden had waited until they were both settled in to have the wedding. During those weeks, when he wasn't working, they'd spent their days looking for a house in the area and making love.

With the wedding only days away, she wanted to pinch herself. She and Jaden had found a cute house that overlooked the stream on the edge of town. It had plenty of room inside and out for the family they were planning. Olivia had spent hours painting and decorating their new home. They'd stayed in the apartment over the sheriff's department, planning to spend their first night as husband and wife in their new house.

Olivia couldn't wait to start her future with Jaden—and put the past behind her. Especially Starling. Unfortunately, that part wasn't that easy. She found herself thinking about all of it.

Jaden had filled in some of the blanks. She now knew why she'd thought she'd seen Elden Rusk the night of the tornado. Emery had put Krystal up to it to scare Rob. Apparently, he owed everyone in town. That he was running away with Angie had come as a surprise.

"He'd been busy keeping his affair with Jenny Lee from her," Jaden had said. "But I wouldn't be surprised if he'd suspected more was going on out at the barn than she'd told him."

Had Dean really not known what his wife was up to? "That reminds me," she said. "It completely slipped my mind until just now. I saw Dean as I was leaving home. He flagged me down on the road. He said he just wanted to give his best wishes to my engagement to you, but after he drove away, I thought it was strange since he hadn't seemed that glad to see me."

"But he flagged you down."

"Maybe only because it was just the two of us on the road," she said. "It would have looked strange if he'd just driven by." Jaden didn't look convinced. "At first, I thought he was on his way to my house, but wouldn't he have turned around and gone back to town?"

"Where did he go?"

"On down the road. It seemed odd until I remembered there was a shortcut back to town."

"Shortcut?"

"It connects to the road to the south." She saw his expression change.

"The road out to Angie's barn," he said.

"Is there any reason he'd want to go out there?" she asked and saw him frown.

She shouldn't have been surprised the next morning when he announced he was going back down south on deputy business. It was a miserable late-November day, the mountains socked in, a mist of rain and snow peppering the windows.

"This is about Dean, isn't it?" Livie said. "I thought the case was over?" He didn't have to answer; she saw the answer on his face. "Jaden, we're getting married tomorrow," she cried. "The rehearsal dinner is tonight!"

Chapter Twenty-Four

Jaden stepped to her, taking her in his arms. "This is what it is going to be like married to a deputy. You can still get out of it."

She sighed and shook her head. "Not this time. I'm in it for the long haul. But please don't make me have to rehearse my wedding alone."

He kissed her. "I'll be back in plenty of time. But it might help if you had the dinner first, then the rehearsal," he said sheepishly. "This is probably just a wild-goose chase, but I've got to check it out."

She gave him the side-eye. "Just be careful."

"I always am."

ALL THE WAY on the drive, he kept trying to put the pieces together. He hadn't told Livie, but the investigation had felt unfinished, as if he'd missed something important.

When she'd told him about Dean, he'd known at least why he'd been feeling that way. Everything about Dean Marsh's story had felt off. But then, the entire Halloween night and the days after the tornado had made it hard to pin it down. So many relationships, so many lies.

He kept thinking about the one question that had bothered him. What if they were all lying?

It had begun to snow by the time Jaden reached the barn property. There was no sign of anyone around. The crime scene tape had been removed, except for a small piece that flapped in the wind by the front door.

He reminded himself that this could end up being all for naught. Yet his instincts told him there was something here to find. He parked and pulled on his coat, drawing up the hood and reaching for his bolt cutters as he stepped out into the weather. These kinds of days were the worst. Wet snow hit his jacket and ran in rivulets.

As he walked toward the barn, he felt the hair rise on his neck. Dean wasn't there, but he'd been here. Not that he'd left tracks in the freezing earth. A new padlock had been placed on the door. It took a little longer to snap this one since it was thicker than the last. It finally gave with a loud snap.

Putting down the bolt cutters, he opened the door. No alarm went off. The crime team had disconnected it so it no longer alerted Cody Ryan of a break-in.

The electricity had been cut off, the barn abandoned, until Angie Marsh could be found and arrested.

He pulled out his flashlight and shone it around the room. He wasn't sure what he expected to find. The interior looked as it had the last time he'd seen it before the crime team had closed up the place. Dean hadn't been in here, he realized. He wouldn't have been able to get past the large padlock on the door.

Still, he'd had to look. Dean could have forced a window. But why would he? He had to have known that the investigators would have found anything of interest to the drug operation. What would Dean have been looking for? The DCI would have taken any drugs, any money, so what else was there? Maybe he'd just wanted to look around, though that seemed unlikely.

Stepping back out into the storm, Jaden closed the door. He still couldn't shake off the eerie feeling Marsh had been out here. Something was wrong. Livie had seen Dean headed this way with a shovel in the back of his pickup.

The wind whirled the snow around him, giving him glimpses of the mountains. It felt too quiet, but then, snow did that. At the sound of flapping of wings, he looked up to see a bald eagle fly past. He followed its flight path with his eyes as it disappeared behind the barn.

He felt an icy chill rush up his spine as another eagle flew by, headed in the same direction. Moving toward the back of the barn, he told himself whatever the birds were feeding on could be the carcass of an animal that had died back there.

But he knew better. His stomach lurched at the scent of rotting flesh as he came around the corner. One of the eagles took flight. The other kept picking at the flesh of the body now only partially buried.

He shooed away the eagle and stepped closer to the body. It appeared a burrowing animal had dug up what had been buried in the shallow grave before the ground had frozen solid. He could see where someone had tried in vain to dig up the body with a shovel with no success.

It would have been impossible to identify the woman's body as Angie Marsh's except for her dark hair. She'd had it pulled up in a ponytail the day she'd been frantically packing to leave her husband. Jaden recognized what was left of the T-shirt she'd been wearing that day. Turning away, he fought the nausea that rose in his throat. Nothing about this case had been easy. He had wanted to believe it was over, everything explained, all the loose ends tied up. But that nagging feeling that he'd missed something had continued to haunt him.

Pulling out his phone, he made the call. He would have loved to have arrested Dean himself, but there was somewhere he had to be.

"Going to also need Dean Marsh picked up for questioning in the murder of his wife."

"Aren't you getting married soon?" the officer asked after Jaden told him what he'd found.

"I sure hope so." He thought of Livie waiting for him back in Fortune Creek. No way was he standing her up. "Send a state trooper as quickly as possible to secure the scene. I have a rehearsal dinner to get to."

Jaden remembered the surveillance camera that had picked up a woman abandoning Angie Marsh's vehicle in Spokane. Dark hair, pulled back in a ponytail, sweatshirt, dark glasses, same build as Angie Marsh.

Then he thought about the rotting corpse. Angie Marsh had never left the valley. Dean had made sure of that.

"Also, you need to pick up Jenny Lee for aiding and abetting a criminal," he said. "She's possibly an accomplice in Angie Marsh's murder. I'll write up my report after I get married."

If he got married, he thought, looking at the time. He was calling it close.

Chapter Twenty-Five

Olivia refused to look out the window one more time. Jaden was right. This was what she had to look forward to being married to a deputy. Wondering if he was all right or if he was dead, killed by one of the bad guys he was so determined to capture. Was she sure she could do this?

"What do you want to do?" her mother whispered. They were seated at the large table in the café. "Alice is ready to serve the meal. Should we wait?"

Shaking her head, Olivia said, "No, we'll go ahead and eat. He'll be here soon."

The sheriff's wife, Molly, reached over and squeezed her hand. "He'll be here. I'm sure he's fine. I've been here before," she said, glancing at her husband. "You just have to think positive."

Olivia nodded. Unfortunately, she couldn't right now. It wasn't even about the wedding. She wanted to see Jaden come through that door. She couldn't bear the thought that she might not see him alive again. Her hand went to her stomach as she thought of the news she hadn't yet told him. She'd been saving it for their wedding night. She was pregnant. They had started their family.

Her eyes burned with tears. She fought them back, lifting her chin. "Yes, let's eat," she said to the small gathering. "Jaden is out saving the world, but we don't have to starve while he does it." Her voice sounded much stronger than she felt.

JADEN SLIPPED IN the back of the café just as Alice started to serve the rehearsal-dinner meal. He'd cut it close, all the way thinking of his beautiful bride-to-be. He hated to let her down tonight. Not that he didn't know there would be other nights. He was an officer of the law. It wasn't a nine-to-five job, especially in Fortune Creek with so much area of the state to cover.

If she didn't realize that, he feared she had tonight as he slipped into the seat next to her. A round of applause went up. He saw the relief on Livie's face and knew he would see that a million times in the years ahead. His job was dangerous and unpredictable and often ran overtime. He'd found his calling after he'd lost her the first time. He hoped the job wouldn't cost him her now.

Her eyes filled with tears as he met her gaze. She smiled, her relief palpable. He smiled back. The group at the table began to clink a utensil against their glasses.

"Kiss! Kiss!" they chanted.

They didn't have to tell him twice. He leaned in and kissed the woman he loved. She put her arm around his neck, drawing him closer. They lost themselves in the kiss for a moment, pulling back when the crowd at the table got rowdy and Alice announced, "Let's eat. We have a rehearsal to get to!"

OLIVIA SPENT THE night in her mother's large two-bed hotel room across the street from the sheriff's office and the apartment over it. It had been their plan to spend the night before their wedding apart, but after her fears yesterday, she wished she was curled up in his arms.

Her mother had already fallen asleep and Olivia found herself at loose ends. After the dinner and the rehearsal, Jaden had told her what he'd discovered.

"You think Dean killed her?"

He'd nodded. "I don't think she ever left for Spokane."

"But I thought you said she was caught on a surveillance camera?"

"I now believe it was Jenny Lee, pretending to be her. It made no sense that she would leave her car to be vandalized, her belongings stolen," he said. "I think he either found her out at the barn or managed to get her out there."

"And killed her." Olivia had frowned. "You're saying this happened when he was allegedly missing after the tornado."

"Angie said he would turn up, and he did. But he must have come back sooner than when he was found walking down the road saying he didn't remember anything."

"Like Cody," she'd said.

Now, as she looked out the hotel room window, she could see the light on in the sheriff's office. Her husband-to-be was busy the night before his wedding writing up his report. Olivia sighed and told herself that Jaden had said there were hardly ever tornadoes, let alone murders, around Fortune Creek.

She could only hope, she thought as she crawled into bed. She was getting married tomorrow. Unless there was another murder.

JADEN HADN'T REALIZED how long he'd been waiting for this moment as he stood at the altar in the church, his best man the sheriff beside him.

"Nervous?" Brandt asked. Jaden shook his head. "Liar."

The music began. He stared down the aisle, waiting for that moment when he would see his bride. Molly Parker came in first, and moments later, there Livie was. He tried to swallow the lump in his throat at the sight of her. She'd always been beautiful, but today she took his breath away as she walked toward him.

He tried to breathe, his heart racing. This was the moment. He looked into her eyes as she joined him. He thought he might see doubts or at least nervousness, but he saw none of it. This woman was going to marry him.

The weight of that didn't help his breathing. Somehow, he got through the ceremony. They'd agreed to keep it short and sweet, and it was.

The next thing he knew, the pastor told him he could kiss his wife. He pulled her to him, their gazes locked, and he knew in his heart that this was the real thing. The kiss drew applause. People in this small town would applaud anything, he told himself as he stepped back, smiling.

Livie was smiling, too, her face aglow. He reached for her hand as the pastor announced them as husband and wife.

FOR OLIVIA, THE WEDDING was a blur of people Jaden had often talked about from his hometown. All of Fortune Creek had turned out for the wedding. The sheriff's department's elderly dispatcher/receptionist, Helen Graves, had brought her knitting bag, working on a project as she waited in the pew. There was Jaden's good friend Ash Holland, from the hotel, and Cora Green, who owned the convenience mart and gas station, and, of course, Alice Weatherbee, who was catering the reception in the hotel lobby. Even the local coroner, J. D. Brown, attended.

There was a huge wedding cake as well as Alice's signature dessert, her famous huckleberry pie. Olivia couldn't believe what a warm welcome everyone gave her. After the stories Jaden had told her, she'd felt as if she already knew them all. But over the weeks preceding the wedding, they'd become like family.

Her mother had cried during the ceremony and again at the reception. "I'm so happy for you," she'd said, hugging her. "Did you know Ash said there is a hotel room open for me, no charge, anytime I come up to visit?"

"You can also stay with us," Olivia told her. "We have an extra room with your name on it."

"That's nice, but the two of you will be honeymooning for the first year," Sharon Brooks said.

"Maybe for quite a few months," she agreed. "After that, the baby might make it harder."

"Baby?" Her mother's face lit up. "Does Jaden know?"

"I'm telling him later tonight," Olivia said and pretended to lock her lips and then her mother's, since she looked as if she might burst with the news.

"I'm so happy for you," her mother said, her voice breaking with emotion. "All I've ever wanted was for you to be happy."

"I am happy," she told her as Jaden approached and a familiar song began to play.

She'd planned to wait until they were alone to tell him about the baby, but the moment she looked at him, heard their song begin and stepped into his arms, she knew she couldn't keep it to herself any longer.

"Having fun?" he asked, pulling her closer.

"It's incredible, isn't it?" she said of the love she felt in the room, saw in his eyes.

His gaze held hers. "Mrs. Montgomery, you're glowing. I've never seen you look more beautiful."

She smiled up at him, then moved closer to whisper,

"We're pregnant." She hadn't meant to just blurt it out, but she couldn't stand it any longer.

Jaden jerked back, surprise and delight in his expression. "You're sure?"

"It's early, but yes. We're going to be a family."

"Oh, Livie," he said, tugging her close. "We're going to be a family."

She shook her head and looked around the room at everyone who'd helped make this day so special before settling her gaze on his again. "We already are a family."

* * * * *